SCIENCE PROJECT

Chapter 1

It's funny how things work out in life. The way things can all seem to come together, and in the end, life is good. For me and this story however, well, let's just say it's so far out in left field that I can safely tell it and no one will ever believe a word. I do need to lay a little groundwork for the first page or so. I want you to have all the facts, some of the facts just needing to be known going in. First off, my name is Tim Miller, even if I do change it later in life. That of course, is part of my story and we will get to it later.

My story begins in kindergarten. It was the first day of school. Mom was so excited as she got me ready for school. The big yellow bus pulled up at the end of the driveway. It had a picture of a big bird in the window. Mom and the bus driver, Miss Wellington, helped me on. I thought the bus driver must be old because she had short hair. And it was blue like grandma's, only a brighter blue. Mom had told me only old ladies wore their hair short and blue like grandma did. You can imagine my surprise later in life to realize she was probably only 20 or so.

I was also told that when it was time to go home, the bus would have the picture of big bird in the window and something about the number 89-1, but all I was hearing was Big Bird. Well, mom was saying big bird and Miss Wellington was saying 89-1. I didn't know any numbers yet, so I listened to my mom. Anyways, it turned out our seats were assigned. So of course, I got stuck next to a girl. Not just any girl mind you, but a cute, red headed one.

She kind of reminded me of my pet mouse Pinkie. Her mouth was narrow, her nose pointed out. She was just plain cute, and I wanted to draw whiskers on her the first day I saw her. That and hold her hand. I mean, I was sitting next to her and all I could think of was holding her hand. Well what can I say, I was only five years old! Well, being only five years old, I was completely lacking any social skills. I also had problems with pronouncing some sounds and letters. So, when she said her name was Renée, I couldn't say the 'R', so her name sounded funny when I said it. She seemed very nice and pretended to help me say it right. Finally, I gave up in frustration when the bus got to school. Besides, the bus driver keeps telling everyone to be quiet. It was noisy, as Renée and I had to yell to be heard.

Oh, I almost forgot about the stops on the way to school. You know, the bus would stop and a new kid or two would get on. Well, not so much the stops, but it was the last stretch of road in the morning. The sun was shining in through the old oak trees that lined the road. Each time the light flickered in Renée's dark green eyes, I became lost in them, they seemed to twinkle in the light. Little did I realize how bad I had it for this girl at the time. It was so bad, my mistake the next day would haunt me well into high school.

All too soon our first half-day of school was over. Thank god it was over. I ran out to the corner where the busses were waiting. Then I found the bus with big bird in the window. Renée was already seated, and I joined her. She had a different teacher than I did, so she hadn't been in my class. The ride home was too short because I hadn't worked up my nerve to hold her hand before I had to get off. However, I was looking forward to the next day of school. It would be the only time till I was a senior that I looked forward to school.

Mom was waiting for me when I got off the bus. I had to tell her about my first day of school. Everything we did, and even why I had finger paint on the end of my nose. Well I had painted a picture of Renée of course, and told her so. Mom must have thought it was cute. She must have figured out I had a crush on the girl. Well, that's what she called it later, anyway. Mom was a painter and I wanted to be one too. I also knew I wanted to paint Renée someday, but I wanted it to look like mom's paintings, not like the finger painting, we did at school.

My second bus ride the next day did not start off that well. Big Bird was gone. Mom was inside, and I didn't know if it was the right bus. Miss Wellington still had blue hair and she told me to hurry up, she didn't have all day. When I said there's no big bird, I heard the older kids laughing at me. I saw Renée looking out the window at me, and I knew it was the right bus. So I got on and found my seat. Now I had been thinking about her all night. Since everyone in our family had nicknames, I decided to give Renée one I could say. Since she reminded me of my pet mouse, I called her Mouse. I mean I gave her a very nice nickname. At least I thought so, anyway. She, however didn't see it that way. She crossed her arms on her chest, looked out the window, and didn't talk to me for the next 3 years. I think she was even crying.

Yes, that's right; we had the same driver and the same assigned seats for the next three years (Three years of hell). Every day I tried being bright and cheery. I got on the bus, found my seat and said, "Hi Mouse", with a big smile on my face and every day I got the same icy cold stare back at me. If looks could kill, I died many times over the next three years.

Oh yes, my speech problems with letters disappeared half way through kindergarten. But the cute little girl named Renée would always be my little Mouse. The other kids liked the name as well, so it stuck to her like glue. Mouse is what everyone called her from the third day of school on. I think that is what really got her mad at me the most. She thought I was making fun of her. I know the way the other kids said it that they were. I felt sorry for her, but no matter how much I tried to say I was sorry, she would just ignore me, when she didn't break into tears, that was.

It was the start of 3rd grade when things changed. A new bus driver, and the seat assignments no longer applied. That was OK with me. I wanted to sit in the back with my friends Danny and Ben. I wanted to take the bumps in the road that almost made our heads hit the ceiling. Mouse stayed in the same seat she always sat in. From now on however, she sat next to a girl named

Lucy. She and Lucy became best of friends. Since Lucy was new to our school this year, she didn't know about our history. When people said, "Hi Mouse", Lucy would set them straight.

The two of them even conspired to give me a demeaning name. "Lonesome Boy" I do not know how they came up with it. But every day I got on the bus I said, "Hi Lucy, Hi Mouse", as I passed, and they said, "Get lost lonesome boy." OK, I was shy for the most part. But lonesome? Hardly. I had lots of friends, and other than a few of the other girls, no one else called me lonesome boy. I finally gave up and stopped talking to her at all. At least it worked until sixth grade.

Renée had gotten braces, and some of the other kids started to call her the 'steel jawed rat'. I think the first time I saw her crying over that nickname, I realized what I had done to her. I wanted so much to tell her I was sorry. But Lucy would never let me get near her to say anything. If I got close enough my ears got abused by Lucy, and even Renée would join in at times. When the braces finally came off in 8th grade, she no longer looked like a mouse. She still had long red hair, but as her body started to change, so did her dress. I swear it looked like her mom was shopping for her at Goodwill. Baggy oversized clothing was all I ever saw her in. It was too bad; I thought she had gone overnight from cute to pretty. Well at least her face was a few grades up from pretty. If she would have just gotten rid of the glasses she had. I mean, come on, they looked like they were donated to the lion's club back in the 50s.

The feud lasted into our senior year at high school. When I say feud, I mean it was a duel. Our entire experience in school pitted our brains against each other. The fight was always on for who got the best grade in class. Sometimes she would even outdo me on a test or a paper. It got real old for me quick in high school. The only thing that made it any easier was the fact that we only shared a few classes together. I mean, we were both smart, but always having her bragging when she got a better score got old. I was also very glad she never took any of the art classes. Lucy tried cheerleading, and the few games I went to, Renée was always close by, cheering her on. This had gone on long enough, that when rumors were going around school that the two of them were lovers, Lucy stopped the cheerleading overnight.

It was unfortunate, because even in middle school I always wanted to ask Renée out to a dance or something. But if she and Lucy were lovers, oh well, I guessed it really was never meant to be. Renée hated me, and I could tell it. It was too bad, because I loved her fiery red hair and deep green eyes. Oh, those eyes, I could lose my soul looking into them, if given the chance. Unfortunately, trying to do so would have cost me my soul if Lucy had been around. Of that one fact I was very sure.

It was the last day of our 1st semester. Our science teacher had given a test the day before and was lecturing us on our science projects coming up. We would be partnered three or four to each group. The project was to be completed in three months' time. The best three groups would go to the regional science fair. In the regional there were scholarships to be had, so my buddies all wanted to partner up with me. Renée had the same problem. Basically, everyone knew that the two of us would get an A for the project, and the project was 50 percent of the semester's grade.

To the class's utter shock, the teacher said that she was going to assign our partners according to the project she assigned to us. Ouch! We didn't even get to pick our project; she was going to assign it to us. She started mentioning all kinds of ideas for different projects, and the subject of robots came up. I think it was Danny that did it. He was a computer whiz and was looking for an easy 'A' I think. Many questions were asked about robots because they had become such an everyday part of our lives. I Mean, we have robot cooks, robot vacuums, even a robot that takes out the trash. Some have two legs and walk like a human and some have four legs and pretend to be a dog. Heck, some of the wheeled models even walked the dog. Anyway, I was deep in thought and was thinking why any of them don't look human.

So I asked my question, "Way don't we have androids by now?" Some of the kids laughed like it was a joke. The teacher was looking at me like I had just asked her a stupid question. And then Renée (Mouse) put her two cents in. She said, "Tim just wants to make a fake girl so he can finally get laid." I was fuming at her for that remark. I mean I was saving myself for the right girl. Hell, to tell the truth, up to that point in time I was saving myself for Renée. The class and even Mrs. Happily laughed at the statement. Well at least until she looked in my face. Then she changed the subject of our discussion to something else.

I never did get an answer to my question. As for Mouse, well, let's just say I wanted to stomp on her and smash her into the ground. I had never hated her before, but now I was thinking of murder as a solution to getting rid of her. Thank god it was Friday. No more bus for me, as I drove to school now. I didn't see the Mouse the rest of the day. Other than our 3rd period science class, the only other time we would see each other was lunch, and I had brought my own this day. Hot lunch sucked when they served their cardboard pizza. So, I avoided the meal whenever I could. There should be a law against some of the food they serve us here. I mean other than the pizza being bad, the only other thing fit to eat was the fried chicken because it was made at a local restaurant and brought in.

It was the following Monday that our world fell apart. Yes, 'our world, ' meaning Renée's and mine. First the teacher had the gall to make us partners. That was bad enough In Itself, as Mouse had not said a civil word to me since kindergarten. Then we got our assignments. Renée and I were given the task of building an android. Somehow, I think the teacher was punishing us. I mean putting us together and then giving us a project that should take years to develop and we only had three months. Then she toldus to split up with our partners for the day and collaborate on a plan to develop our projects.

Our first drafts in the projects were due next Monday. Crap, Crap and Double Crap was all I could say. What was Mrs. Happily up to? I had never known her to be mean to me before. She had never been mean to Renée. After all, since we started High School she had treated Renée like a pet; Teacher's pet, that is. I knew for a fact that Renée sometimes helped her grade papers. Mine would come back to me with an extra big red mark and a circle around it when I would miss a question. I just knew it was Renée's doing because Mrs. Happily always used small red check marks.

Mouse and I found a corner and glared at each other for a minute or two before she broke the silence. Mouse asked, "Why did you ask that stupid question yesterday?" "Me!", I responded. "You're the one that took the jab that resulted in us being partnered up." "You're the one that asked the stupid question.", She stated quickly.

"I don't know why anyone would think a question was stupid. My dad always tells me the only stupid question is the one that goes unasked.", I said.

She seemed to think about it for a few moments. Then "maybe" was all that came out of her mouth.

I told her, "Well, I am not the one that verbally attacked you in response to your question."

She looked like she was considering it for several moments. To my utter surprise Mouse was the one to offer an olive branch.

"Well, I am sorry I did that now." She apologized adding, "But it looks like we are stuck with each other. Worse, we have an impossible project ahead of us. So, I will tell you what, if you don't call me Mouse anymore, I will stop calling you lonesome boy."

"And?" I prompted.

She looked at me and said, "All right, no name calling of any kind."

What could I say; I mean after all how hard could it be to stop calling her Mouse? I hadn't said it to her in years. Besides getting her to stop cutting me down the rest of the year would make it well worth it. So, I held out my hand and said, "deal." And Renée said "deal" then took my hand to shake it.

Chapter 2

All I know for sure was that her soft, small hand was so warm to the touch that I forgot to let go. Funny thing is she didn't say anything about it. She just started to talk again.

"I am sorry about the fake girl remark by the way." Renée apologized, "It was incredibly mean of me."

"Yes, it was." I agreed.

"Well the steel jawed rat was very mean of you to come up with", she said.

"Renée," I said as I looked into her deep green eyes, "I didn't come up with that one. In fact, I never ever called you that."

I was afraid she was going to let go of my hand. I could feel it tremble a bit. So, I added quickly, "I am sorry I ever gave you that nick name. It probably is what gave the other kids the idea in the first place." Her hand stopped trembling.

She was looking me in the eyes and said, "I have waited a long time to hear you say that, I'm sorry I have been so mean to you all these years."

"Oh, don't worry too much about it.", I replied, "Building a sex bot would be child's play compared to this project."

"What do you mean?" she asked.

"Simple, take a model 2 robot frame, glue on a rubber dildo and voilà," I said, "instant sex bot."

Her eyes got real big. She looked like she was considering what I had said, then asked, "You think that would work?"

She looked flushed as I thought about what I had just said.

I said, "Yes, you could program the robot to move like a real person and it would work."

Then she uttered, "Oh shit", then said, "Excuse me" and she was off for the little girl's room.

I know that was where she was heading because she grabbed the hall pass from the desk. Mrs. Happily, our teacher, always had a bathroom pass sitting on the desk; it was made out ahead of time, just in case someone needed it. Renée was gone for about 10 minutes, and the whole time I was left on my own to think about the project. I had an inspiration, and I shared it with her when she got back to class.

"Look," I said, "Mrs. Happily can't really expect us to develop a Hollywood style android with an AI brain in three months."

"No shit", she said, but I didn't feel like she was swearing at me.

"So, I was thinking, if we built a robot that was human looking in detail and..." I said, trailing off trying to figure out how to say the last part when Renée blurted out.

"You mean anatomically correct right?", She asked.

"Yes, anatomically correct is the best term.", I answered, "Anyways, we can mostly use off-the-shelf parts and put them together. Make a human mold from a casting and then incase a robot in silicon and make it look as close to human as possible."

"Yes, but what about the AI brain?", Renée asked. "I mean that's what would make it an android right?"

I answered, "That's the best part, we can just say that as soon as AI technology is developed, we will be able to upgrade the android to full capability. Besides, my question the other day was only dealing with the looks, not the full function of an android."

"You really think that would get us an 'A' for the project?", she asked.

"Yes", I said, "she can't really expect us to create an AI brain in three months, can she?"

"Not without putting Chris Weston on our team she can't.", Renée stated forcefully.

I surged, but it was true, that girl might just be able to pull it off. Then again that was her project, AI computer systems wasn't it? She would be real competition at the fair. Not to mention her boyfriend Jim. I really wonder what he would come up with. Undoubtedly it will be something out of this world if I have learned anything about him over the last year or so.

"All too true, and why is that?" I asked, "I mean all the other teams have four people, we are the only two-man team."

Renée shrugged in total confusion.

I asked, "You don't think she really intends to fail us the last semester of our senior year, do you?"

"Well, I wouldn't think so.", She answered.

"Right," I said, "so instead we create the android body and then leave the AI brain to Chris and the experts."

"What if that's not good enough?", She asked looking more than a little concerned.

I said, "Then we can talk to the counselor about her giving us an impossible assignment for the purposes of failing us."

"Oh, so where should we start?", Renée asked.

"Well I am going to spend the night on the net trying to find out everything I can about androids.", I said.

"That sounds like a plan," Renée said, "I will do the same."

"Oh, well here then, let me give you my email and you can forward anything interesting you find.", I said.

"OK, well I guess I had better give you my email as well.", She replied.

I looked at her email and smiled saying, "Hey, we both have Hotmail, we can IM the information back and forth."

"That would work.", She said.

Oddly I could swear I saw a gleam in her eye. 'Stop it, ' I told myself, 'she really does not like you.' The class period ended, and we went our separate ways. Lunchtime, well hot lunch today was going to be fried chicken. The cafeteria didn't fry it. They had a contract twice a month with a local restaurant to fry it up for us. It was delivered hot and was really one of the best meals they served here. So today was going to be a hot lunch day.

Lucy and Renée were already settled as I walked by. I almost couldn't resist, but I remembered my promise, and as I was going by I said, "Hello Lucy, Hello Renée."

Lucy looked like the world had just fallen on her head. All that came out of her mouth was "Heeelllooo" and that was kind of weak sounding.

After I got passed the table I did hear Lucy whisper to Renée, "What's wrong with lonesome boy today?"

I did not hear Renée's answer. Well my deal was with Renée not Lucy. Maybe I could come up with something to call Lucy. Wait, Peanuts, yes that would work. With her shoulder length hair, she reminded me of the cartoon strip character anyways.

I got my lunch and sat down to eat with my best friends Danny and Ben.

Danny asked me, "So what's the deal with the tornado twins?"

They really don't look alike; Lucy has raven black hair after all.

"Oh, you mean them." I said, "Well I made a deal with Renée and we are not going to call each other names anymore."

Danny said, "Well darn, I guess it's been fun while it lasted."

"How's that?" I asked him.

"Oh, come on, you and Mouse have been fighting, like, like forever like." Danny said, "If it's over, then the rest of our senior year is going to be boring."

"Hey, when did I ever say anything bad about her?" I asked.

Ben spoke up just then, "Hey, if you two are going to be nice to each other, maybe you can take her tothe prom."

Danny laughed so loud at the ridiculous idea that everyone was staring at him. He looked around and said in too loud a voice, "Ben thinks Lonesome Boy and Mouse should go to the prom together."

The laughter that erupted around the room with that suggestion made me feel about two inches tall. How did I ever get a friend like Danny anyways? Then I remembered it was a long time ago and he was a very different person now.

I caught Renée's eye and she looked at me. She had that you broke our deal already body look about her. I shook my head no and pointed at Danny. She rolled her eyes. I hoped that means she believed me, then she turned back to talking with her conspiratorial friend.

Finally, the school day was over, and I went home. I had a feeling it was going to be a long night.

I spent the evening on the Internet. I live in the basement of our house, no one comes down here but me. Well mom does to do the laundry, but most of the time I have the basement to myself. I even have a bathroom of my own. It's only a four-bedroom house and there are 6 of us kids. I am the oldest, so guess who rated when dad finished off the basement. I never understood why my parents didn't just buy a bigger house.

Like I said, I have my own room with my own bath, complete with a Jacuzzi bath tub big enough for four people. Dad has his own plumbing company and the tub was returned because the customer claimed it was scratched. Right, you couldn't see any scratches on it, but because it was a custom order Dad couldn't return it. Anyway, when he was finished with the basement, I got the tub because he didn't know what else to do with it. My bathroom and bedroom were roomy. The rest of the basement is divided into a utility room and a rec room that no one else uses, so I used it as my private studio. I sculpt, paint, and I also draw. But my real passion is sculpting.

I sat down before my computer and signed onto the net, I began my search for information on androids. I was rewarded; I found lots of good information on androids. Unfortunately, none of it was useful to me. The IM window opened showing that Renée was on. I almost lost it when I saw the IM screen picture that showed up. She was using one of Minnie mouse.

'Well maybe she did like the name after all.' I thought.

I waited a while to see if she would IM me. She didn't. I decided to check out eBay and see if anyone was selling a model 2 cheap. I was thinking of that model because it walked on two legs and was small, about 5 feet tall is all. It was lightweight and most of all it should be cheap because they had been out for 14 years now.

I found a boxed lot offered for sale in the local area.

I read the ad, 'Parts from ten model 2 robots, no CPU. Larson salvage.' OK then the opening bid was $10.00 and there was 6 days left in the auction. I decided to IM Renée and send her the page link.

She typed asking, "Why did you break our deal?"

I typed, "I didn't."

"But Danny called me Mouse.", She typed.

I typed, "But I didn't say it."

She replied in all caps, "BUT DANNY DID!!"

"Renée, did you make a deal with me or did you make it with Danny?" I asked typing.

Before she could respond I typed, "You know Lucy called me Lonesome boy at lunch. Does that meanyou broke our deal first?"

"Ah..." she typed.

"Yes, I am keeping are deal. How about you?" I sent her next.

"I'm sorry, you're right, you and I have our deal. Not me and Dandy boy." She replied.

"LOL" I typed.

"Grin smiley", She returned.

Then she added, "So how did the prom get in this?"

So, I typed, "They asked what the deal was between us, so I told them. Then Ben said that if we were going to be nice to each other I should take you to the prom. Danny thought it was a good joke and the rest you already know."

"So, are you planning on asking me to the prom?", She typed asking.

'Oh shit, here we go!' I thought, 'The loaded question that I have no way to answer without getting deep into trouble. I mean, yes, I would love to take my dream girl to the prom. But there was no way I was going to ever ask her, given our history. Why do girls have to do this kind of thing to me?"

I typed, "You want me to be honest?"

"Yes.", She typed back.

"I don't think I have a chance in hell of you saying yes if I ask." I typed in return.

She typed, "Oh..."

Then I got nothing for about 15 minutes.

She came back, "Sorry, Lucy logged on and wanted to chat."

"That's OK," I replied, "did you look at the auction?"

"Yes, but what good are the robots without a CPU?" She typed back.

"I have an old XBOX III here." I replied, "We could use that CPU. It's the main chip they use in most robots."

"OK, go ahead and bid on it then.", She typed.

I suddenly realized that money could be a problem here. Not for me, dad would just give me whatever I needed for a school project. But Renée, I didn't think she had any money. I mean she always wore clothing that looked like it came from the Goodwill. Then I decided that I would never ask her for a dime. It seemed like a good idea at the time. So, I dropped a bid of $100 on the parts.

Then I typed, "OK, I put a bid in on the parts."

She typed "How much?"

I replied, "Enough."

"LOL, male chauvinist I will just let you pay for it by yourself then." She typed back.

So, I typed "OK, you can be the model for the mold then."

"WHAT!?!?!" She typed.

"We need to make a casting of someone. I don't know about you but paying a model to do it will break the bank." I typed.

"Just a second," She typed, and then added, "Lucy sent me this link, you may want to look at it."

The link followed. I clicked on it and found I was looking at a sex doll site. What the fuck is this? Damn that Lucy anyways. She is trying to say I need a doll or something. I was fuming mad.

So, I typed, "So what am I supposed to do with this?"

She typed in return, "Click on the link for order info first."

I typed in, "I just know I am being set up here."

She typed back, "No trick, you have to see what these things sell for first."

So, I clicked on the link and holy shit, these things sell for $25,000.

I typed "25K, holy shit! That has to put a serious ding into someone's pocket book."

She typed, "I just wanted you to see the price. Now click on the making the doll link."

I did and hit pay dirt. They had a step-by-step guide on how they made the doll. Right down to the name of the silicon they used for the molds.

She typed in, "They even have a link for a video of the process."

I clicked on it next.

She typed, "You watching it yet?"

I typed, "It's loading."

The video was 22 minutes long and even showed someone using the female doll at the end. Strangely I was feeling horny from the last few minutes of the video. When it finally finished I typed, "Wow! Pay dirt."

She typed, "Here is a link for the male doll video."

This video was only 12 minutes and showed three women using the male doll for their fun. OK shit, now I got horny after watching it! Three women and a male doll, lucky doll I thought. Why can't something like that happen to me?

"You still there?" she typed.

"Yep, I am here, barely." I typed back, still thinking of those lucky dolls.

"I know the feeling; can you keep a secret?" She typed.

This is getting strange. I mean she is talking about what I feel like, and what she feels like?

But I typed my reply to her question, "Is it illegal?"

"No." She typed.

"Is it immoral?" I asked typing.

"Maybe." Was her reply.

'Well this should be interesting' I thought.

Finally, I typed, "OK, I will keep it a secret."

"Lucy's dad has two of these dolls." She typed back.

"NO SHIT?" I returned.

"No shit." She typed.

"I am floored." Was all I could reply with.

"You are probably jacking off after watching the three hot babes." She typed.

I looked at the screen in disbelief. What is she fishing for here?

"LOL" is what I typed. What the heck, it's not like everybody doesn't do it after all.

She sent me another smiley grinning again.

Then she types, "Daddy's home; got to go now. Bye."

Then she disconnected from the IM.

It was getting late and I decided that I needed to use the Jacuzzi. I was horny, and there's really nothing like jacking off in a tub of hot swirling bubbles. As I sat naked in the tub, I was thinking of Mouse. I wondered what she looked like under her clothing. Shortly I found myself masturbating to her image. The image changed to that of a doll that looked like Renée, then of the real Renée and then back to a Renée doll. It did not take long and then holy shit!! That was the strongest orgasm I had ever had.

I went to bed that night and had a dream about Mouse and Peanut playing with the male doll. And guess what, I was the doll. When I woke I found that it had been a wet dream as well. Odd, I thought, I haven't had a wet dream since I started masturbating.

Chapter 3

Class was normal today. Anyway, I was in a bit of a shock when Renée asked me to join her for lunch. We sat together and talked about the project. She then asked me why I thought she had to be the model for the mold.

I told her it was simple. "You see, my stature is too large to fit over the frame of a model 2, whereas your smaller size should be the perfect fit."

She frowned, and then said, "I was hoping we could make a male android."

"Oh, I see, I suppose Lucy wants to buy it for herself when we are done."

"Cha-ching!" said Renée.

"Just joking", I grinned.

"I wasn't, you know ... if your idea worked, we could get rich selling robotic dolls on the Internet."

I thought that over for a minute. Customers pay 25K for a plain doll. Those look real. But they don't even move by themselves. Our product would create a new niche on the market, the leading class. We would define the standards! Oh yes! Definitely.

"I wonder what people would pay." I absentmindedly said out loud.

"More than you think, I bet", answered Renée.

OK, she had me here and I knew it. She was right. Program the frame with some human looking movement routines. Now, how did she put it? Ah yes, anatomically correct! Well then our androids would probably sell like hotcakes.

"Are you proposing we go into business together?" I asked.

"Well, only if you really do ask me to the prom."

I was speechless, staring at her forever. Damn! There was that glimmer in her eyes again, so it seemed to me, anyway. The bell rang, sending us to class. 'Saved by the bell' was all I could think of as I walked away, and for some reason I thought that was unusually funny.

That afternoon I logged on the computer to find eight emails from Renée. Each one was a link to a different site. She had been a busy girl after school.

The first link was a supplier of silicon. They had all grades and even sold the dyes to make it the color you wanted; available in one or five gallon sizes and even in a 40 gallon barrel. The other links were equally interesting. A company that sold latex suitable for art grade modeling cast. It was on an art supply site. Another link proposing 'do-it-yourself dildo kits'. "Make a mold of your own cock!" I sneered. Great! What would I do with a mold of my own cock? I got a devilish grin. Could I sell it to Lucy? Hmmm!

Next link was leading to a plastic mold company. They had a do-it-yourself plastic shell that you could wrap upon any object to fit its contours, nicely following each and every nook and cranny. One then filled the shell with liquid resins to make a hard cast mold. It was perfect for what we were planning.

Renée's last email had a project price break down.

Robotic Parts?

Molds $200.00

Liquid latex $25.00

Silicon and hardener $125.00

CPU Free.

Miscellaneous $50.00

It looked like we were up to $500 for the project so far, that is, if everything went all right. This according to "Murphy's Law" never happens. So I took dad's advice

'Take your parts cost and double it, then you should have enough to handle any actual cost overruns.' This would put the cost at a whole grand, all for a school project! Methinks my Dad might just balk at that. However, if we just ... I became distracted by what I thought.

"Just what does a new model 2 sell for anyways?"

Just one way to find out quickly. Google to the rescue. And after the quick search I found they were selling new for an average of $2500. Ouch! Well that was my first impression. However on further thought, what if we actually went into production?

Let's see! Molds were a onetime cost. And all we would really need after would be the silicon and the model 2. So we could build those things for about $2800.00 each. If sold for the same price of $25,000 each, that would mean a unit profit of $22,200 each. It got me thinking--dad works 10 to 12 hours a day and makes about 125,000 a year. So I would have spend about 80 hours on each android. A total of two weeks for each from start to finish. That means, I could make 23 of them in a year. 23 times 22,000 equals 506,000 for a year. Not too bad! If we could sell the androids for twice that price that would be a million. By the time I split that with Renée, we would each make 500,000 a year. Wait! If Renée would help me build them, then we could make them twice as fast, so that would be one each week. And if we were able to...

An incoming email interrupted my thoughts. It was from Lucy and read: "I am having a birthday party for Renée at my house next Friday night. She will be 18 years old then. You are invited. The party will be from 6 p.m. until 9 p.m. for the boys."

I wondered what she meant by the boy part, then remembered that my parents had let my sisters have a sleepover. That must be what was going on. But why would Lucy invite me? What the heck, just ask. I typed my answer:

"Lucy, are you sure that Renée would want me there? Tim."

As I went back to formulating my plan to get a grand out of dad, the IM window opened. The graphic of the peanuts character showed up in the picture view window. It was Lucy.

"Hi Tim."

"Hello Lucy."

"I think you should come to the party."

"So you're sure you want me there? Why?"

"Am not sure myself, but it would make Renée's day."

"What do you mean? I don't understand."

"Tim are you blind?"

"No. I don't think so. Why do you ask?"

"Renée is in love with you."

That sure shocked the hell out of me! Renée, in love with me? Never had I heard such nonsense. That was ridiculous, that was ... preposterous! Unheard of, silly, even. That's interesting, claimed a little voice in the back of my hard skull.

I answered after a long time--testing the water, so to speak.

"Lucy, you're lying to me, aren't you? I mean, I smell something fishy here, Renée hates me, has for years!"

"No, she loves you. I don't lie, I swear!"

"Well, it's hard to believe, you know. Up until yesterday, she wouldn't even talk to me unless she was cutting me down."

"That's because of the horrible fun you made of her and that nickname you gave her. Why did you name her Mouse, anyway?"

"Sorry--that's kind of personal!"

"The doctor is in," smiled Lucy. Or I imagined her smiling anyway.

"LOL" I typed

"Now tell me, please? No charge! "--Lucy again.

I was laughing so hard that I couldn't resist.

"Are you going to pull the football away at the last minute if I tell you?

"LOL. No, no football."

I typed, "Promise never to tell?"

"Cross my heart. The needle in my eye and all that stuff."

"OK, it's like this. When I was five, I had this really cute pet mouse named Pinky. You weren't around then--you came only three years later, so you don't remember when Renée and I first started school together. You see, I couldn't say the letter "R" back in those times, so I finally gave up in frustration. Anyways all my famlly had nicknames for each other. So I picked her a nickname, one of the cutest things I could think of. Since Pinky didn't fit I settled on Mouse."

"Tim, are you telling me that you called her "Mouse" because you thought she was cute?"

"Bingo, you win the Kewpie doll."

"Oh shit. Damn. I ... I would never have guessed that in a million years."

I couldn't resist so I typed. "Down the hall second door on the right."

"Thanks a lot."

“Don't mention it.”

“Tim, you're not pulling my leg are you?”

“Just about the bathroom location. I have never been in your house. Otherwise, no, I don't. That's the whole story, plain and sad.”

“I think we need to talk.” typed Lucy after a brief hesitation.

I send back: “Isn't that what we are doing?

“Tim, do you still think she is cute?”

“Lucy, she went past cute in 6th grade. Now she is so hot that, well let's put it this way ... She's beautiful, she's gorgeous. And she's brilliant! She made me really happy yesterday when she made the deal to be nice to me.”

“So are you going to ask her to the prom?”

“Why would I do that? Besides, she would just tell me ‘No’.”

“I am pretty sure she will tell you ‘Yes’.”

“Oh, that's right--you told me she was in love with me.”

“She said since you were 5.”

“She wasn't even talking to me when I was 5.”

“That's because she thought you were making fun of her with that nickname.”

“But I wasn't.”

“But that's what she thought.”

I froze. Was I talking to Lucy? Or was I talking to Renée? Maybe with Renée and Lucy at the same time. Either way this could be interesting. I mean, I could have some fun with it. Then again did I really want to make things worse? Not really!

I typed, “Lucy, I have been in love with Renée since the first day I saw her. I gave her a special name that meant the most to me at the time and she rejected it. I have never said one mean thing to her in all the time I have known her. No matter how many mean things she said to me. Now you expect me to believe that she has been in love with me just as long? I can't believe that. She hates me and the only reason she is being nice right now is because we can't work together on this science project if we are putting each other down all the time."

"Tim she is in love with you. I thought you were making fun of her all these years."

"Lucy, I don't believe it. I also don't think it would be a good idea for me to come to the party."

"Tim, what can I do to convince you that you should come?"

Interesting, the places I can go with this. Well, what would I like? An apology from Lucy in front of the lunchroom might be a start. Maybe with a kiss thrown in. No, the only girl I want to kiss is Renée. I have dreamed of that day since I was five. Well, OK I was a little older than that, but holding hands at five should be about the same thing, at least that's what I think. On the other hand I wasn't so sure about who I was talking to. I mean, if it was Renée, or Renée was with Lucy, then I didn't want to mess this up. So in the end I wanted more time to think this though.

I hastily wrote, "Let me sleep on that. I will let you know tomorrow."

"Okay then, Tim. See you at lunch tomorrow."

"Bye..." I typed.

"Bye bye".

I switched my IM status display to 'off line'. The connection was broken a second later.

Shit! I thought to myself. What if that's all true? Or what if it was really Renée I was talking too. Or maybe I was talking to both of them at the same time. Shit, this is a fine kettle of fish. I would have to tread very carefully. After all I didn't want to make matters any worse now, did I?

Chapter 4

Renee has been eyeing me all day in class. I thought I saw tears in her eyes a couple of times. Then again maybe that is just wishful thinking on my part. I mean, I didn't want to hurt her. Besides if she was crying over this, which meant at the very least, Lucy told her what I had said. I really didn't think she would keep it secret from her. Heck, there was a rumor that the two of them were lovers.

Lunchtime finally came. When I got to the lunchroom, there was a gaggle of girls at the table with Renee and Lucy. Since there was no room and Renee looked so unhappy, maybe it would be better to sit elsewhere. So I headed to the table with my friends Danny and Ben. No sooner had I sat down than Danny started in on me.

Danny said, "Dude, what did you do?"

"What are you talking about?"

"Guy look, Renee has been crying all day. Every time she sees you or anytime someone calls her mouse, she breaks down in tears."

"I don't have the vaguest idea what you're talking about. I haven't even talked to her since lunch yesterday."

Ben "Heads up Tim, here comes Lucy and she sure looks pissed."

Lucy started in halfway across the lunchroom, "You asshole, what did you say to Renee?"

"What are you talking about?" As soon as it came out of my mouth, Lucy was at the table and I felt her open hand smack me. It was right across the face.

"Ouch, that hurt," I said, as I was holding my cheek in my hand. Then the PE teacher, the coach, grabbed me by the collar from behind. "That will be enough of that stuff," was all he said before he dragged me off my feet towards the office. So here I am flopping around, trying to get back on my feet. I wasn't having any success at all and could hear Renee wailing in the back of the room. Even as Mr. Handily jerked my body by the collar, I thought he must have been part pit bull. Buttons were popping off the front of my shirt as he continued to drag me to the doorway. POW, My head hit the doorframe and it was lights out time.

I awoke sometime later in the hospital emergency room. Mom was hovering over me like a wet hen. Well I didn't see dad, and since mom works here it made sense that she would get to me before dad did. The ER nurse said, "I will go get the doctor now.", and she left the room.

Mom said, "What happened, what did you do?"

"Mom, I was eating lunch and Lucy came over shouting at me and then she slapped me. Then that gorilla PE teacher grabbed me by the collar like a pit bull and dragged me from the room. He didn't even give me a chance to walk, he just dragged me until smack, my head met the doorframe. Then I woke up here."

Mom, "That's not what Mr. Handily claims happened."

"Mom have I ever lied to you?"

"No son, I can't say that you ever have."

"Well if you don't believe me, you can ask the other kids in the cafeteria at the time."

The doctor came in just then and came over and checked my eyes with a light.

Then he said, "It's a mild concussion, the x-rays show no cracks. We will keep you over night in the isolation ward and release you tomorrow to the police."

"What?" I said.

Mom looked at him in disbelief.

He didn't answer, fact is he just turned, then walked out of the room muttering something about punk scum and juvenile delinquents. Shortly after he left, the door opened back up and two police officers came in and one of them started to read me my rights.

My mom was outraged, yelled, "What's going on here?", To which the larger cop backhanded her, then twisted her around and cuffed her.

"Hey stop that", I started to say but the other cop's nightstick was quickly against my throat. The smaller one then said to me, "Do you understand these rights, Maggot."

I couldn't talk, hell I couldn't breathe but somehow I nodded a yes.

"I need to hear you say it. I can't hear you.", he shouted in my face and pushed the nightstick tighter against my throat even as the other cop was pulling my mother from the room. Just then my dad arrived in the doorway. Now dad is a big man. He is 6 foot 6 and 300lbs of prime beef. The cop said, "Move it or you will be under arrest as well." Dad was not stupid. He held up his hands and moved back into the hall. Mom was crying and I am sure dad could see the welt on her face. It must have taken all his control not to do something.

The cop by my bed then removed his hand from the gun.

Dad got a big shit-eating grin on his face out in the hallway.

The other cop said, "Can you handle the dirt bag Jason's arrest while I put this one in the car?"

I asked, "Who is Jason?"

The cop said, "Don't be funny maggot. You are and we aren't going to let you get away playing that amnesia thing. He then grabbed my wrist and slapped the cuffs on it and put the other end on the rail of the bed. "I am placing you under arrest for the murder of office Weldon Glazier. Now maggot, you look just stupid enough to ask for a lawyer. You know what happens to cop killers when they ask for lawyers, don't you?"

The other cop had dragged my mother out in the hall and I could see dad on his cell phone. Well, no he was not talking on it. He was taking pictures with it; then again I thought dad's phone could stream video with sound.

I said, "Oh,""Some how I think you are the one that is going to need a lawyer."

Wham. His nightstick came down across my diaphragm and lower ribs. I felt the ribs break even as the wind was knocked out of me and I hurt quite badly. All the air was expelled out of my lungs from the force of the impact. Worse, I found that I couldn't breathe.

My dad yelled, "Now that's definitely police brutality if I have ever seen it."

"Shut up, clear the hospital or I will place you under arrest, too."

Dad said, "My son is a minor and you can't separate me from him for questioning. I have a right to be here and report your abuse as well."

God I still couldn't breathe, with all the pain I was gasping for air.

The cop said, "This maggot is twenty and you have no rights ... wait, what's that in your hand?" He had his gun out and pointed at my dad.

Shit, I couldn't breathe, mom had just been arrested, they thought my name was Jason and Dad was about to get shot by the cops. Could this day get any worse?

Well, only for me. However it was going to get more interesting here in a moment, because the nurse picked that moment to walk into the room. She looked confused and then she demanded, "What's going on here?"

The cop looked at her standing between dad and him like he couldn't believe she was doing it.

The cop yelled, "Out of the way. That man behind you is armed."

She turned and looked at my dad holding a cell phone pointed in the room.

Then she said, "What is he doing, calling a lawyer or something like that?"

The cop, "He has a weapon in his hand."

The nurse said, "He has a photo phone in his hand. And what are you doing in this room anyways? The man you're here for is up in surgery. And by the way, they don't expect him to live though it.", she added.

The cop said, "This isn't Jason Copper?" He pointed at me.

The nurse looked at me and saw I was turning blue in the face.

"No he is a head trauma case from the high school. What have you done here, why is he turning blue?"

The cop said, "Oh Shit. But the old doctor out there just said our man was in this room?"

The nurse was over to my side in a flash. I don't know what she did to my stomach because everything was turning dark the same moment she touched it. I did however feel a sharp pain just before I passed out.

Chapter 5

Later I woke up in the hospital recovery room. There was a large bandage over my stomach and an oxygen mask over my face.

"You feel better now?" said a nurse.

I said, "No" in a raspy sore voice.

Then she said, "Well you are a lucky young man because this happened to you in the ER. If it you hadn't been here when it happened, you would be dead right now."

"Great" I said.

The nurse said, "Well the surgeon had to remove the broken rib that was pressing against your diaphragm. I am sure he did a good job, but then I am kind of partial to my husband's work. Also I came up here to make sure no one else mistook you for someone else."

Ok, she was sweet in a motherly kind of way.

"My parents?"

"Your dad is going to bring your mother back from the police station. From what he told me on the phone she is going to need to be treated down stairs and then she can see you in your room when we get you out of recovery."

"Thank You." Was all I got out?

She said, "So you're Tim are you?"

I nodded a yes.

Hum, "You sure now how to get in trouble, don't you?"

"It seems to find me. At least today it does."

"Yes, I was just looking through your records here, it doesn't look like anything has ever happened to you before."

"No, today has been quite bad."

"So any other bad days?"

"Not really."

"School going ok, you're a senior aren't you?"

"Yes."

I think I got this figured out; she is trying to get me to say something or talk so that I stay awake.

"Any girlfriends?"

"No not really."

Come to think of it, she looks like someone I should know.

"Any possibilities?"

"Not really."

"That's too bad, a big handsome young man like you. I would think the girls would be falling all over you."

I smiled, "They do that. But I am not interested in them."

"Oh? You like girls don't you?"

"Yes, I like one girl. In fact she is what started all this."

"Tell me all about it." Here you don't need the mask anymore." And she took it off me.

I sang like a bird. I told her about Renée, the email the pet name and about how my day had gone from bad to worse. Even that I was a virgin and was planning on waiting for the right girl.

"How's the pain now?"

"About a 5 I think."

"OK, the sodium pentothal is wearing off, let's give you something to help with the pain."

"Thank you, nurse."

"Betty, Betty Rainer."

With the shot in the IV I fell asleep, thinking about Renee Rainer.

Mom and dad came into my room later to see how I was doing.

Betty came in to see me often. She was always nice and talkative. She seemed really interested in my hobbies. I even did a rough cartoon sketch of her and her husband. It was ok, not my best work. But hey, with the pain and all I couldn't move the way I normally would have. Apparently they liked it a lot, because I saw it hanging in a frame behind the nurses' station on one of my walks.

The day before I was released Betty gave me a few pictures of Renee from summer vacation. She said that I should paint her as part of my recovery.

I was shocked when I looked at them. She was naked on the beach. Then Betty said, "They're from the Sunny Side Naturist Resort, we go there every summer."

After three days, I was released from the hospital. It's too bad dad has to sue the hospital. They were awfully nice to me and really went out of their way to make sure I was comfortable. Dad says that he has to sue them to sue the doctor that misidentified me to the police. Oh we are suing them as well. I understand that the police officers are suspended and will probably lose their jobs. The one may even be charged with attempted murder. Dad says that the city has already offered $100,000 to settle this quietly. Our lawyer gave the city a copy of the attack video from dad's cell phone and the lawyer said they changed their position as soon as they saw it. He also gave the news media a copy just so they couldn't claim it was faked, or something like that anyway.

Jason, the cop killer they mistook me for, died, I suppose getting shot in the head will do that. I just didn't want to leave a loose end here just in case you really cared. I know I don't. I never owned a gun and never thought I would need one. Dad had a shotgun, however it was old and he never used it. It was mounted on the wall in his den and I don't think it even worked.

As you have already guessed, it turns out that Nurse Betty is Renee's mom and she spent a lot of time with me during my stay. Renee is not poor, the clothing and eyeglasses she wears are an act. They're her way of keeping the boys at school away. Her dad works at the hospital as well, chief surgeon and much to my gratitude the one that saved my life. Oh before I forget, his name is Tom.

I found out I had been expelled from school the day I got home. The school was trying to press charges against me for starting a riot and resisting a school official. Seems they couldn't get the police to arrest me for some reason. I was left with the impression that the police wanted to stay as far away from me as they could. Our attorney said that he talked with the county prosecutor and there was no way they would even consider prosecuting me. The PE teacher had some kind of history of unnecessary roughness in the school system. And that was before he even knew about the hospital incident.

Our lawyer, Mr. Airdack, served the school papers later that afternoon - Reckless endangerment of a minor and assault resulting in injury. Also we are suing the PE teacher.

Well anyway with my expulsion I will be getting out of that school project. Most of my friends came to visit me in the hospital. A few said they would stop by my house and see me when I got out.

I tell you I got the biggest kick out of the TV news people. They filmed me leaving the hospital and then had more at our house when we got home. I guess being almost killed by the police in a hospital bed handcuffed to the bed is news worthy. I don't understand why myself. I hear cops are always arresting innocent people and making their lives a living hell. Why should I be any different?

It was a week before I managed to sit down and sign on my computer. 327 new emails. Great, I wondered what are they trying to sell me now. More Viagra, or maybe breast enhancements. Like I need breasts. Then there is always the penis enlarger. Why would I want to make it bigger? Isn't 9 inches long enough? I tell you if I had a nickel for every spam email I got, well, let's just say I would be a millionaire right now.

I started looking at the sender names.

Not much in the way of ads here. Let's see most of my friends have emailed me at least twice. There was an email from Lucy and 23 of them from Renee. I decided it would be best not to read those 24.

There was one about winning the Ebay auction. It was from the man I had won it from. He said he had seen me on TV; at least he thinks it was me. See what I get for using my real name for my email account. He said that when I got a chance to, and not to rush, I should just call him or send an email. He also mentioned that he would be glad to deliver my auction items under the circumstances. Seems I won the auction for only the 10 bucks. I clicked on the link and paid him with my online account. Told him I was housebound for the next week, but when he had time he should just call ahead so I could have someone there to help him.

He called me within an hour and came over two hours later. He had 21 boxes of parts altogether. He even carried them down to the basement for me. I have no idea what I am going to do with them now. After all, being expelled from school, I was not going to have to worry about a science project, now was I?

I spent an hour answering the emails from my close friends. Danny and Ben being the big ones. I was sore and tired after that so I got up from the computer and lay down on the couch in the recreation room, turned on the TV and selected the Sci-fi channel. I was rewarded with the Stargate SG1 marathon. I think I made it through two episodes before I fell asleep.

I have been home for two weeks now; the doctor came by the house today. You guessed it, Renee's dad. He said I could go back to school on Monday next week. I told him I was expelled and would not be returning. He was red-faced when I told him why.

Dad got a call a few hours later from a lawyer that specializes in children's rights. He told him we had a lawyer and gave him Mr. Airdack's name and number.

I was sitting outside the house on the porch. We had one of those old-fashion deck swings, you know, the ones that hang from the porch and have more than enough room for three people. I was sitting on it, in the cool weather of that late March afternoon on Saturday, when Lucy came up the driveway. Oh crap, all I need now, I thought.

She came up on the porch and said, "I was hoping you would have accepted my apology in the email.

"Haven't read it yet. I had over 300 emails when I got home last week. I still have over half of them to get through." I was hoping she would leave.

"Tim, I am sorry I slapped you. I didn't know what was going on with you and Renee. I mean I didn't know she was talking to you under my account."

So it really was Renee I was talking too. My mind raced with that little bit of information.

"Lucy, You're forgiven." Ok I was flustered and just wanted to get it over with. Beside I never could win a disagreement with a girl.

"Really?"

"Yes really."

"Are you going to email Renee?"

"No." I said a bit too forcefully.

She looked perplexed.

"Does she need to come by and talk to you?"

"No Lucy, I don't want her to come by. Look I was expelled from school and am not going to be going back there."

"They expelled you for nearly being killed?"

I can't believe this girl.

"No, they expelled me to try and cover up for Mr. Handily manhandling me without just cause."

"Oh, aren't you going to fight it?"

"Dad has a lawyer working on the lawsuit right now."

"I got a three days' suspension out of it you know." When she had that 'I know something you don't know look about her.'

"No, I didn't know that."

"Yes, right after they took you away in an ambulance the principal had me in the office to find out what happened and suspended me for three days."

"Really, that's interesting. Are willing to testify to that in court?"

"I guess, why?" She seemed like she wanted to say something else but didn't.

"They didn't expel me until three days later. What you just told me proves it's a cover up because they knew the truth beforehand."

"Yes I will testify, will you please talk with Renee, she is beside herself over all of this."

I thought of that for all of 3 seconds. I didn't want Renee beside herself. I mean hadn't I caused this girl more than enough problems in life already?

"Tell her she can come by sometime if she wants to talk."

Then Lucy shocked me. She kissed me on the cheek where she had slapped me. "Thank you" then she ran off. I watched her go in absolute amazement. There was even an extra wiggle in her walk. Lucy had never wiggled before. And who would have thought that Lucy Martin would have ever kissed me? Not me that's for sure. And Renee has been in love with me all these years. I just sat there in silence as my worldview was overturned once again. It was a long time I sat there. I was sore and tired when I finally got up. Somehow I made it inside and down to my room. I just wanted to lie down.

Chapter 6

The next day I was sitting in front of the computer and called up Lucy's email. I was almost in tears before I was done reading it. It was eight pages long and describes how she had been wrong about me all these years. And yes, she was the reason that Renee treated me so bad. She was the one that had encouraged Renee to do that to me. And yes she agreed Renee did look like a mouse. Somehow I thought that the email did a much better job of explaining things then Lucy had done upstairs yesterday evening.

I was going to look at Renee's emails next when I heard the doorbell ring. Shortly after that Renee came down the steps and walked into my room.

I looked at her and she looked at me.

"I am sorry about all this," she started. But I put my finger to my lips and hushed her. I stood up from the computer and stepped over to her. I didn't even stop to think about what I did next. I put my hand to her cheek and lowered my head to kiss her. Oh sweet Jesus, what a kiss it was. She melted away to nothing in my arms as the fireworks exploded all around the two of us. I just held her a bit, enjoying the moment before I spoke. "I still have a pet mouse as cute as you are," I said. She started to bawl and bawl in my arms. My shirt was getting quite soaked. Finally I was so tired I couldn't take standing any more.

"I need to sit down, I am getting tired."

She nodded, and then helped me over to my bed. I sat down and she sat next to me.

"Tim, did you really mean it when you said I was cute as a mouse?"

"Yes, but you grew up on me."

"And what am I now?"

"Gorgeous, my dear little mouse, just gorgeous."

"Ah."

She kissed me again. Long and wet, her tongue slipping in to duel with mine. My mind was defiantly in sync with my little head; at least both of my heads had the same idea. Too bad the rest of my body wasn't up to the task. Of course there was no way she could miss my hard-on if she looked down. It was tenting my sweatpants rather obscenely at the moment.

"Tim, Is all that stuff you told my mom true?"

"Yes, every word of it. But I didn't even know she was your mother until later."

"So you have been in love with me since we were five?"

"Yes I have."

"You can call me mouse anytime you want to."

She pushed me back in the bed and started to kiss me again.

We heard an "Ah humph" from the door. My dad was standing there.

I looked at him and he spoke.

"I just thought you would like to know you are un-expelled from school. I just got off the phone with the lawyer and the school board has settled out of court. Mr. Handily and Dr. Thomson are being terminated as part of the deal. Also the school system is paying you $100,000 towards your college tuition. It seems that a girl named Lucy was suspended for slapping you the day you went to the hospital. Her affidavit proved that there was a cover-up. The school board just wanted to settle it quietly after that came out."

"Wow."

Renee asked "What about the police?"

My dad said, "That is a different suit altogether, it is going to take some time I am afraid. The good news is we did settle for a $100,000 for your mother's false arrest and injuries. I think they were afraid that your testimony on the stand would end up costing them a lot more."

Renee, "And Tim's?"

"Well the city has offered $1,000,000 as of yesterday. I haven't had time to ask you if that's enough Tim. I mean it's going to be your call after tomorrow when you turn 18 anyways."

I shook my head, "It's not about the money. Let me think about it. Maybe I need to talk to that lawyer again and see what he suggests. What about the hospital?"

"That's a long one. Looks like we will have to take the doctor and them to court."

Renee, "That's too bad."

"You're right, we would have settled for the $250,000 offered by the hospital but the good doctor will not go for it."

"Doctor Williams wants to go to court?" Renee wanted to know.

"Yes he does. He doesn't feel he is at all to blame for the police's mistake. He said and I quote him, young punks have to learn not to drive motorcycles in their schools."

I said, "Is he for real?"

"Personally, I think he is off his rocker."

Renee, "I better tell dad about it."

My dad said, "And thank him for the attorney he got to help with the school system."

Renee, "I will."

And then, to my utter surprise, dad left. I mean just like that he left. I looked at Renee and she looked at me. I then noticed that she wasn't wearing her glasses.

"So where are your glasses?"

"Well a, well I don't wear them when I am not at school. You see, I don't really need them."

"That's what your mom said."

"She did?"

"Yes she did."

Renee looked around like she wanted to change the subject quickly.

"She also told me about a little girl that was madly in love with a big mean ogre."

"Oh." Then her eyes fixed on the photos on my wall.

"Where did those photos come from?"

"I took them."

"Wow, I didn't know you were so, ah, artistic."

"We have never had an art class together."

"Right, I am not any good with art. Well not painting or drawing anyway. I never have tried taking pictures."

"Don't worry about it, you belong in front of the camera not behind it."

She blushed. "So you want to take my picture do you?" It was said in a tone that left no doubt she was asking me.

"Nope?"

She pouted, "You don't?"

"No, I want to sculpt you?"

She gulped "You sculpt as well?"

I smiled, "Out in the rec room, on the far wall. Come I will show you." I was still sore, but I manage to get up. And took her out to the rec room and her mouth dropped open. There were busts of my parents, my three sisters, two brothers and even one of me.

"You did all of those?"

"Yes, but dad says I need to get his a toupee."

She got on her tiptoes to see the top of his bust. Then she started to giggle. Did I tell you she was only about 5'4"? Probably not, but compared to my six feet she did look small like a mouse.

"And the paintings?"

"Guilty as charged, but I like sculpting the best."

She looked at the six portraits hanging on the wall. And then she saw the easel with the drape over it.

"What is this one of?" She asks.

Ok, do I make something up here or should I let her look at it?

"You promise not to get mad if I let you look? I mean it's not quite done. I have only worked on it a little since I got out of the hospital."

"So way is it covered?"

"Well, your mom gave me a picture of you from summer vacation and I didn't want my brothers to see it."

"It's of me?"

Then her eyes went wide. "Did you say summer vacation?"

I nodded yes.

She went over to the easel and slowly lifted the canvas tarp. Then she stared at it for a long time. I was really getting worried about what she would say or do next.

"Are my breast really that big?" she asked.

Maybe the question put me in a better mood. I mean I was getting worried because the picture was of her on the beach at the Sunny Side Naturalist resort. But I said, "Well they look that big in the photo, but now that you're here we could have you pose and make a comparison."

She looked at me and smiled. Then she lifted her sweatshirt up over her head. I stared at the lovely sight before me. "Yep, they are really that big. Let's see, B-cup, I think. But to really be sure I would have to go into sculptor mode and get a hands-on feel for things."

She gulped, "Yes."

"Yes?"

"You better make sure," she said in her shy voice.

And I did make sure. Her warm breasts fit very nicely into my hands.

She moaned softly at my touch. My hands were encircling her fleshy mounds; I so wanted to kiss them at that moment.

The sharp pain in my belly reminded me I was not ready to be active yet. I grimaced at the pain. Renee saw me and became concerned.

"Maybe we should save this until you're feeling better", She said in a pouty voice.

"Maybe, but I don't want to." I grinned at her.

She pulled her sweatshirt back down and smiled, "When you're better! For now we just talk."

I put on a pout face then, "Can we kiss?"

Smiling as she says, "Yes.", she bent her head up to receive one from me. The kiss lasted an eternity, complete with fireworks flying everywhere at the same time.

Mom called down, "Tim, is Renee still down there?"

"Yes" I yelled back up to her.

Odd, mom didn't say anything back for a while. When she did it was, "OK, get decent, we are going out to Baja with Renee's parents."

I said, "All of us?"

"No, just the six of us."

I looked and Renee and she shrugged her shoulders and did that thing with her eyes, telling me silently that she didn't know what was going on either.

"What for?"

"Your birthday is Monday and her parents have to work that evening."

"Ok we are coming up."

"Don't forget your coat and tie dear, they have a dress code remember?"

How could I forget? I only get to go to the exclusive seafood place once a year. You guessed it, for my birthday.

"I need to swing by home for a dress", Renee called upstairs.

"Hang on", Mom called down.

We did, walt that is.

"Your mom says she will bring it over and you can change here. Oh Tim, Betty wants to know how you're coming on the painting."

Renee chimed in, "Tell her it's almost done."

"I will dear."

Renee turned to me and said, "Well maybe we had better get you changed."

We went into my room and Renee went to my closet. I only had one suit so there wasn't much of a decision only whether or not to wear the vest. I felt my stomach and decided not to wear the vest for some reason. Mom always hung the suit with the shirt that went with it so it was a no brainer until she looked at the tie rack.

"Loony Tones" she said with her eyebrow raised slightly. I think she was just questioning that I had it. Not that she thought I would want to wear it at the moment. So seeing an opportunity to play the straight man I said "No not today." She giggled and then looked at the assortment of ties. She held one up to suit and nodded, "You approve of this one then?"

I said, "Perfect." It was a plain blue tie. It was the one that went best with the blue-grey suit.

Renee was every bit as efficient helping me dress as her mother was the day I got out of the hospital. Soon she was even tying my dress shoes. It was a good thing because bending was really hard on me. Best of all I didn't even have to ask her to help.

As soon as I was done Betty and my mom June were down the stairs in a flash with Renee's dress.

Betty, "Here is your dress honey, go change. And you handsome, Can I see how the painting is coming?"

"Yes, it's out in the rec room." Mom led the way as Renee went into my bathroom to change. Somehow I didn't think it was fair that I couldn't watch.

"Oh, my God", my mom gasped with her hand over her mouth.

Betty asked, "I thought you said it wasn't finished?"

Mom sputtered, "You don't mind him doing a nude of your daughter?'

Betty smiled, "No, I gave him the photo of her that he has painted and wow is all I can say! It looks better than the photograph."

Mom was dumbfounded. She was rather conservative on the nude issue. She might have made a bigger deal out of it but she was a painter herself. I must admit though that she has never done a nude that I know of.

I said, "Thank you, I just need to work on the background some."

My mom uttered, "You gave my son a naked picture of your daughter?"

Betty said, "Oh it's just a snapshot from summer vacation, it's no big deal."

Her comment left mom speechless. I know mom didn't approve of nudity like that. I had heard her comments, all negative, on the NIS (Naked in School) program that was the rage in California. She worried about it going national.

Betty, "Oh, I see what you mean about the water needing some more work."

"Yes, I think I got the sand down."

Renee came into the room then. She looked stunning, radiant, and absolutely gorgeous.

When I turned my head towards her, I was left speechless. Our mothers on the other hand started chattering a mile a second. It didn't take long and we were upstairs, out the door and on our way. The moments seemed to pass in a blur. I don't know for sure what was said during the drive. I spent my time getting lost in her eyes.

When we arrived at Baja I was let out of the car at the door with the women. Normally I wouldn't do that but my ribs were still sore. I was shocked when the maitre d' motioned our group to a table. The restaurant doesn't normally take reservations despite the princely prices on the menu. It turns out that they didn't take a reservation, but they did recognize me from all the TV coverage. Well I didn't like all the attention, but I didn't mind this VIP treatment. Besides how many people really have their rights violated by the police in error. I am really beginning to wonder about that. Renee's father and my dad were surprised to find us seated when they came in from the car. There was still quite a line of people waiting to be seated.

We waited for the waiter making the normal chitchat that polite people do. When Tom, Renee's Father, said that it this was the least he could do since I was not able to come to Renee's party, I also learned that Mom and Betty were good friends. Must be because they work together. I mean they have never socialized together before, at least not that I know of.

Dinner was good; I had lobster and crab legs I could eat. Renee even ate more of the crab legs then I did. The subject of school came up and Renee and I both expressed concern about our science project. We had already lost three weeks because of what happened with me. Tom thought I would have to be an artist to pull off making the mold. He didn't know about the painting or my love of sculpting.

Mom looked rather perplexed about the idea of us building an android. She really did think it was a waste of time. Dr. Rainer and Dad were thrilled with the idea as was Betty. Mom didn't actually say anything but I knew the look in her eyes. She disapproved of the idea. Then again she disapproved of me getting a computer, video game system and just about anything to do with technology. In a lot of ways, she was very traditional in her thinking. Then again, she didn't seem to like me doing nudes either. That could be what it really was about I thought to myself. Dr. Rainer and Dad offered any help they could.

Well Renee's late birthday celebration as well as my pre-celebration was over too quickly in my opinion. We even got two cakes that the place was famous for. No way six of us could even eat one. We were stuffed to the gills with seafood already. Altogether it was fun and I even forgot about my discomfort for most of the meal.

Chapter 7

Monday Morning,

It was my birthday, well other than the normal hugs and kisses from mom and dad; we had already celebrated my birthday on Saturday. But even so I still had to return to school. I was surprised my parents let me drive to school. But that wasn't the only surprise: the mire fact that I was returning to school so soon after starting the lawsuit. Well dad explained time critical lawsuits take priority. That and the run in with the police didn't hurt at all for speeding things up. Besides this deal was struck outside of a courtroom.

Upon entering the school I was immediately sent to the new principal's office. Her name was Dr. Clare Rumbskin. She was about 60, silver haired and she didn't know how to smile. Talk about how to make a bad first impression. This woman could give lessons. Oh maybe that's why she went into teaching in the first place.

"Well young man," she started, "I will not tolerate any misbehaviour from you. You are to consider yourself on probation for the remainder of the school year."

"Pardon?" I asked.

"Don't give me that innocent routine. I am not happy that the school board has ordered an expelled student reinstated. I checked the report of your PE teacher and I have no doubt that you are a disruptive influence in this school."

"Maybe we should be having this conversation with my lawyer present."

"That kind of threat will not work with me young man."

"I wasn't making a threat ma'am, it's just that my legal council said that the terms of my return to school were without restriction."

"Are you calling me a liar here?"

"No ma'am, I am however wondering if I shouldn't be calling him for clarification."

"That does it, you are suspended for three days. If you want to go for an expulsion again, keep it up."

I got up and left her office. I went to the payphone to call my father when she came up and slammed the hook down. "Get out of here or I will call the police and have you arrested."

One of the secretaries spoke up, "Dr, Rumbskin, that would be a very bad idea."

"Shut your mouth, if I want your opinion I will ask for it." Sheesh I thought this woman does not know how to make good impressions on people.

I shrugged my shoulders at the secretary and started to walk away. I heard the doctor say to the secretary, "Draw up the expulsion papers, that boy is not going to be allowed back in my school."

Talk about unreasonable people. As I was exiting the school I ran into one of my lawyers. Well the one that was handling the school system problem. Talk about covenant. His face turned bright red when I explained what happened. Apparently the principal saw us talking outside and had called the school officer to have us removed from the premises. He came out of the school and over to us. I recognized Officer Clayton and remembered that he didn't know who I was. I guess that's a good thing. Come to think about it that has to be a good thing. Well then again maybe it wasn't.

"I am afraid I am going to have to ask you to leave the school property immediately." The only thing lacking in his voice was any kind of hint he was sorry at all. Actually in light of everything that's happened I'm surprised he came near me. Then I realized that maybe him not knowing who I was might be a problem after all.

My lawyer, his name was James (what a name for a lawyer), introduced himself.

"Officer Clayton, (He read the name tag) I am the attorney for this young man. I have official business with the school here today. Are you telling me that you are going to block an officer of the court from carrying out his duty?"

Clayton, "You may be what you say you are, but I have my orders to remove the two of you from the premises. So are you going to go quietly or what?"

"I see, we will go quietly, but I must also inform you that this action you have taken will probably cost you your job." It must be a lawyer thing; they have this uncanny need to be confrontational. I could have told him it would be a mistake to say that. I mean you could just read it in Clayton's eyes. He looked like a man that had to be right even when he was wrong.

Officer Clayton moved fast. He wasn't going to put up with someone else being right and him not. He had James handcuffed and was leading him out into the parking lot. "I am placing you under arrest for trespassing, failure to obey an officer and whatever else I can think up." That had to be the dumbest thing I ever heard a cop say to a lawyer.

The cop must have forgotten all about me. I made my way to my car and got off school grounds. As soon as I got out of there, I got my cell phone out of the glove box and called dad.

Dad called the other lawyer who said that he would handle it all. He must have done so. I didn't think lawyers worked that fast. But by noon both my lawyers and the school system superintendent were leading me back into the office of the school.

"Rumbskin was furious to see me and called the school police before she even saw the superintendent of schools, her boss as a matter of fact.

"Dr. Rumbskin, what are you doing?" asked the superintendent.

"I am doing my job, that's what I am doing."

"Do you understand you have just invalidated the school system's agreement with this young man?"

"We should not be making deals with slimy young punks. I want him out of my school and I want him out of here now."

Officer Clayton walked into the office just then. "You again, I guess you didn't learn your lesson the first time."

Before he could make a move on James however, Mr. Airdeck produced a restraining order from his pocket and handed it to the cop saying, "You might want to read this before you make a big mistake."

"What the hell is this?" Clayton asked.

"That sir is a federal restraining order barring you from interfering with any of the named individuals on that list from conducting business on school grounds. You will note the names are myself, Tim's attorney James and of course Tim here."

Officer Clayton looked like steam was about to escape from his ears. His face was so red I was sure we would see blood vessels popping any moment.

"How the hell did you get this?" The sarcasm was dripping from his loud voice.

"Well it's like this, a federal judge took extreme exception to my unlawful arrest. You see you were interfering with official court business this morning."

"You're asking for it."

"Paragraph 3 specifies that if you approach within 100 feet of any of the named individuals for the next 6 months it is a violation and you will be held in contempt of court."

"Contempt this", he started to say when he moved forward on James only to have the superintendent of schools step in front of him.

"Out of my way!" he shouted.

"Officer Clayton you are relieved of your duties in this school system."

"You have no right to do that." he spat back.

"Oh I do have that right; I decide who works in my school system and who doesn't. Now you just go report back to your office for reassignment."

"You can't do that, I work at the discretion of the principal of this school."

"Oh, that is no problem; I am now the acting principal."

Clare shouted, "What?"

"You heard me, you are relieved of your duties effective immediately."

Clare, "I have a contract, you can't just fire me."

"I didn't fire you, I merely terminated your current assignment. I am sure we can keep you busy as a substitute for the duration of your contract."

"Well I never, you can't do such a thing. I will see you in court over this."

"You are welcome to try."

Clayton, "You are going to regret this." He was staring the superintendent right in the eyes.

"I already do, now both of you off the grounds."

Clayton looked like he was going to do something rash. But the realization that there were so many witnesses caused him to back down.

"Oh Officer Clayton before I forget." He handed him another paper, "You have been served."

Clayton looked at the paper and turned white this time. "You're joking." He got out. It was the lawsuit against him for false arrest. The lawyer knew what he was doing, I guess?

"No officer, we will see you in court. Now I suggest you get out of here."

Clayton turned and left, saying "you are going to regret this."

Then the superintendent turned to Dr. Rumbskin and said, "Your turn, out."

She was cussing up a storm as she left. She was not as quiet as Clayton was.

"Now, that we have that cleared up, let's get Tim back to class and we can get back resolving the suit as planned."

That's when I found a hall pass in my hand and I was heading down the hall. The bell rang signifying the period's end. Well so much for lunch.

Chapter 8

I got some strange stares from the teachers the rest of the day, but none of them said anything directly to me.

As I was leaving the school Renee and Lucy caught up to me. They wanted to know what happened, so I told them the events of the morning. Both were shocked in disbelief at the way things were happening in my life.

Renee said, "We should go somewhere else to talk about all this."

Lucy, "My place would be good."

So next thing I found myself doing was heading to Lucy's house. Her dad was at work and no one else lived with them. Her dad had been divorced years ago.

Lucy started, "So what can I get you two? Maybe some Cokes?"

Renee, "That sounds good."

I agreed.

Lucy was off into the kitchen. Renee pointed to a leg settled in a chair in the other room. It looked like a woman's leg.

"That should be one of her dad's Dolls."

Lucy walked in, "Oh, that's the new one that he got yesterday."

Renee giggled, "Can we see it?"

Lucy, "Sure, just don't tell anyone about them. I mean I don't think dad would care one way or other, but if the other kids found out at school..."

I spoke interrupting her, "Not from us they won't."

We moved into her dad's master bedroom to find three lifelike silicon dolls there. Two were lying on the bed and the new one was sitting in a chair with her head turned towards the bed were just like she was watching the action. The dolls on the bed where just lying there. It looked like there was room between them for a body.

Lucy said, "Dad loves the things for some reason."

I said, "And it doesn't bother you?"

Lucy blushed a little. "Well, he kind of, well..."

Renee, "He promised her he would buy her a male doll when she turned 18."

Lucy, "Renee, you are not supposed to tell anyone."

Renee, "Tim will keep it to himself, won't you Tim?"

I said, "Oh, sure; who would I tell anyways?"

Lucy, "Ok, well someone might think I am perverted if they found out I wanted one."

Renee, "Well, we are going to go in the business of making androids, maybe you can buy a copy of the Tim Doll." She grinned like a cat.

"Well maybe a male doll, I don't think that Lucy would want one that looked like me."

Renee, "I don't know about that, I wouldn't mind one that looked like you."

Lucy laughed, "I will settle for a dildo copy of your penis."

Now it was my turn to be red-faced. Talk about a surprising revelation. Just as I was going to dismiss it as a joke, Renee said, "I get the first one."

I think I went from red-faced to purple-faced just then. Renee kissed me on the cheek. Then she said, "Well, maybe Lucy would volunteer to be a mold for one of our models in exchange for a copy."

I decided it was time for a change in subject. "Well I am surprised that you can see the seams in those dolls." I didn't want to talk about sex dolls. But it was the first thing that popped into my head.

Renee, "You think we can do ours without a seam?"

"Not sure, but I think I can get rid of most of them."

Lucy, "I got the kits in the mail Saturday."

Renee, "You have them here?"

Somehow I was sure I was not going to like this. I knew I didn't like the sounds of it. What could it mean? Well let's just say my worries were confirmed in a few moments.

Lucy, "Yes, come on I will show you."

With that we were off to the other end of the house. Lucy's bedroom was filled with Peanuts Cartoons of Lucy, who else.

"The postman delivered them on Saturday."

"Delivered what?" I asked.

She pulled two boxes from her closet. They both said 'Do it yourself Dildo Mold'. I must have gone catatonic because. Renee was shaking me.

"Hum, oh sorry" was all that came out?

Renee, "We said if you let us take molds of your penis then we will both be molds for the sex androids."

I nodded dumbly. I mean I think I agreed, but I am not sure. I was in a daze over what was happening here. That and I couldn't believe it. The next thing I knew I was being led to Lucy's bathroom. They were planning on shaving my private parts. What could I say? I was in a daze. Before I knew what was happening my pants came down.

"Hay, he is already shaved," said Lucy.

"What, Oh no, I just have never had any hair grow down there."

Renee, "Cool, it looks so smooth, like a baby's bottom."

Lucy, "So why is it so small?"

Ok, that comment snapped me back. Think! Think! Here I am in the house of the girl I love's best friend, my pants are down around my ankles, and they want to know why my dick is so small. Got it, I think.

"Well it needs to be made interested."

Renee, "Oh it's not interested in me?" She asks coyly.

My cock twitched.

She placed her finger across the top of it. "Oh, I see it needs attention."

I gulped.

Lucy said, "You give it some attention, I will start mixing this stuff up so we can make a mold of it."

Renee, "Tell me if I am doing this right, I haven't ever actually done this before."

"Ah, you're doing fine..."

She was moving her hand up and down on my shaft. Her hand was soft and oh so delicate.

"Oh, slow down or you're going to get ... Oh shit," I came all over her.

"Oh, did I do that?" Renee said with a smirk on her face.

Lucy, "No, he's shrinking. Oh shit, this is going to be ready in 2 minutes. Quick, get him hard again."

Renee "How?"

"How should I know? He is a guy, guys are visual, so show him something."

"Oh, Ok"

With that I watched her strip. It worked. I got hard again.

Lucy was pouring the goop into some kind of tube. The next thing I know she is sticking it over my cock. Well it was a casting after all.

I said, "I hope we didn't forget a step?"

Lucy looked panicked and double-checked the instructions.

"Oh my god we forgot, the baby oil."

"Somehow I think we have a problem here."

Renee, "Maybe it will work anyway."

I said, "Only if we are lucky."

Lucy, "It will only be another minute."

"Does it say what to do if the latex sticks?"

Lucy, "Yes, it says Ouch."

I lost my erection instantly at that news. And yes it was sticking to my dick.

I said "Oh shit."

"Does it hurt?" said René.

"Not really, it is just uncomfortable."

"I'm sorry" Lucy added.

"Well what does it say about getting this stuff off?"

"It says we have to use acetone. I don't think we have any of that."

"Nail polish remover." I suggested.

"Oh, I have plenty of that."

Lucy then opened up the medicine cabinet and took out a large bottle of their polish remover. She opened the bottle and was about pour it on my dick when she stopped abruptly.

"Maybe you should climb in the tub first."

I nodded a yes, and then almost tripped over my pants around my ankles. However Lucy and Renée grabbed me keeping me from falling. Only a little of the polish remover spilled, mostly on me.

Renée said, "Careful I don't want him hurt anymore. Let's finish undressing him before we put him in the tub."

"Okay" I said, as I nodded yes.

Shortly René was removing my shoes and my pants. Lucy was lifting my shirt over my head. When they had me naked they guided me by the hand into the tub. Generous amounts of acetone, the nail polish remover that is, were then added to my nether regions. Fortunately it didn't take long until all evidence of the fiasco was removed. Of course with all that scrubbing by the two girls I was once again rock hard.

"I think he's ready to try again." Said Lucy.

Renée wasn't so sure and she looked me in the eyes. But she was asking me if it was okay.

"I guess that'll be okay but let's take it a little slower this time."

Both girls nodded in agreement. Then Lucy started to read the instructions from the beginning.

Step one: remove all hair from around penal area.

"Well that's already done," said Renée as she looked at me with the question in her eye.

What could I say so I blurted out, "it just never grew there. There is some medical name for it but don't ask me what it is right now."

"Step number two: cover penal area completely in light oil. (Baby oil recommended.)"

"I think that's a step we missed." Lucy said.

Lucy then grabbed the baby oil form the medicine cabinet. Then she started squirting it all over my cock. Both Renée's hands and then Lucy's started to rub it in. Of course my dick responded to their touch.

I added, "If you two keep that up, we are going to have another problem."

They giggled and Renée said, "Well, you did want to take longer."

"Okay, and step three says: mix the latex and partner in container provided for one minute."

"Shit, the mold is ruined, it's full crap." Lucy said.

I said, "You have another kit. Open it and get the other mold."

"OK, I wasn't thinking." said Lucy.

"No you probably weren't." I said as I looked down at Lucy's hand on my cock, stroking it."

"Sorry I just can't get over its size." Lucy smiled at me.

Renée giggled, "Well it is bigger than your strap-on."

"I am surprised as well."

"Don't look so surprised Tim, you knew we were best of friends." said Renée. "And we share everything." Renée and Lucy started giggling again.

My mind screamed, and I can't believe this. I mean here I am standing in the middle of the bathtub completely naked. The girl I love is playing with me while her best friend mixes up a concoction to make a mold of my cock. And then my love tells me they share everything.

Question to self, did I die the other day?

Oh hell I thought to myself, just enjoy yourself; there has to be millions of men out there that wish they were in just this kind of predicament.

At this point I regained my senses. I was able to think and act my normal self once again.

"Everything?" I asked.

"Everything!" Renée confirmed.

"We're ready for him try again" said Lucy.

She poured the concoction into the mold, brought it over and René helped her slide the mold over my cock.

I decided to add, "for that shouldn't Lucy be naked too?"

The girls giggled.

Lucy then said, "Oh, you need more visual stimulation." It only took a moment and she too was naked before me.

My eyes went wide, my cock grew even harder and I had to resist the temptation to thrust in and out of the mold.

Renee sensed what was wrong and said, "Hold on, if you're good maybe I will let Lucy finish rubbing on that thing when we are done." She pointed to what was inside the mold.

Lucy said, "You only need to wait two more short minutes."

"You'll get yours," I said, "When it's time to make a mold of your body."

"She gulped, then said, "Promises, promises, that's all boys ever make to me."

Renee was laughing then. So was I.

Lucy announced. "Time's up."

The two of them started to pull. In unison they announced, "It's stuck," and then they tried to pull it off my cock again.

"Suction", I said. "I need to shrink so that air can get in around it.

Renee got a glimmer in her eye. It was a mischievous type of grin on her face, the type that makes a man worry.

She reached down and oh shit, the shower water was cold. It splashed all over me and guess what, it worked because I shrank and the mold dropped away from my body.

I managed to shut off the water as Lucy claimed her prize. Renee giggled again at my predicament. "Oh, poor boy, here let's make the water hot and get you washed up.

She was as good as her word. In a few moments I was between two naked girls getting soaped up by delicate hands. My cock responded again. And Lucy was the one that was rubbing my cock up and down in her soapy hands when I fired off this time.

Renee, "Well, finish rinsing and we can oil it up so that it stays nice and soft."

We did, and soon I was led into Lucy's room. She had a queen size bed and the girls had me lie on it. Their hands started to roam over my body and they applied lots of baby oil to my body. Fact was, their hands put oil in places that had nothing to do with the process they had just used me for.

Lucy got up and retrieved the mold. She also collected the kits and returned everything to her desk.

Renee said, "What are you doing now?"

Lucy uttered, "Why making the dildo of course."

I said, "No fair."

"What's not fair?" said Lucy.

"Well you are going to have a copy of my dick."

"And your point?"

"I want to at least see you use it on yourselves."

I got a playful slap from Renee on my arm. Lucy looked thoughtful for a moment. Then Lucy said, "I guess that would be fair. But the instruction says we have to let it cure for 12 hours first."

"That means tomorrow then." I said with a grin.

There was a sound from the garage. Lucy's dad was getting home early tonight.

"Shit, he must have left early to spend time with his new toy." Lucy cussed.

"I hope he is not mad about my car in his driveway?" I said. Then I realized that I was naked in Lucy's bed. Somehow I thought the car was the least of my problems.

Chapter 9

Home » Authors » Timm » Science Project » Chapter 9

Chapter 8 Bottom
Chapter 9
Posted: 7/18/2014, 12:18:54 PM
We scramble to get dressed. Renee had to help me some; I still had a little pain trying to bend over. That's when we heard, "Lucy how many times have I told you not to clean your nails in the house? Oh!" He said as he stuck his head in her room. I didn't realize you had a boy in here."

"Sorry Sir." I said.

He looked around the room and the dildo kits caught his attention. He grinned, "I see, now I know way you are apologizing."

The three of us turned a few shades of pink at that.

I stuttered some but he just raised his hand stopping me. He smiled then said, "don't worry about it. It's Tim right?"

"Yes sir."

"You 18 yet like my daughter here?"

"Today sir."

"Well that would explain some of it. Well anyway if my daughter talked you into doing it I'm not going to complain about it now."

With that he turned and left. Renée, Lucy and I exchanged looks of disbelief with each other.

Lucy said, "He must be anxious to get to his new doll."

The girls started to giggle at that, and I join them with my laughter. Thank goodness we all managed to get dressed in time.

We decided to break up our little party. Of course I went home thinking about what had just happened to me. It was so unbelievable, I mean the two girls that had been the meanest to me throughout school. The two vixens just jack me off and it was wonderful.

I briefly wondered just where all this was going to lead.

Tuesday.

Basically school was uneventful today. Our science teacher did spend a few minutes with Renée and me going over our science project since we were so far behind. As it turns out she was impressed with our current plan of attack. She was pleased to find us working so well together. If she only knew just how well we were working together.

Lunchtime was spent with Renée and Lucy going over the building of the android. I'm not really sure how Lucy became involved in this. But I wasn't going to complain as we could use the extra help. The discussion soon turned to marketing anatomically correct robotic sex dolls. Personally I would've preferred that we were talking about building androids but at last current state of technology would not allow us to incorporate an AI brain. The three of us decided that we should meet at my house and see what we could do with the parts we are ready had.

It wasn't long after school that Renée and Lucy showed up at my door. Soon we were busy sorting parts. And we began the assembly process of the robotic frame.

Lucy said, "you guys I don't mean to be a drag, but this assembly looks a little too big to me."

I said, "Drat, I forgot about that 360° swivel."

Renée started to giggle then she said, "I don't think it'll hurt for a male robot, but isn't that protective plate over the pelvic area going to be a problem on the female?"

I rolled my eyes to the top of my head. To which both girls responded by giggling.

"Well it looks like we have to play robot surgeons." I said.

The girls started to giggle then. Oh well, at least I was enjoying their laughter.

"Renée started, dad was talking to me after we left restaurant Saturday. And he said he was going to get us some information on joint replacement components. He seem to think that to do this right the first time, the best way to proceed would be to make the skeletal system of the robot match as closely as it could with the human."

I said, "Yes, that makes sense I don't think we had time to do that for this science project."

Lucy said, "Are the two of you serious about going into business and building these things for real?"

"Only if Tim, actually asks me to the prom." Renée said in a voice that almost sounded like a plea.

Okay this was going rather fast for me. I mean one day I don't think this girl can stand me in the next she keeps dropping hints about going to the prom.

"Okay" I said, "I'll bite." Renée will you please go to the prom with me?

"Well Gee, I don't know Tim, you sure you'd want to be seen there with me?"

"Yes!" I said like I was confused.

"Making him get down on one knee and ask", said Lucy just before she started giggling.

"No that's for something else he can ask me later. Besides it would be too hard to get him to stand back up."

I approached Renée, took her hand and decided to do it right.

"Renée, would you please do me the honour of going to the prom with me?"

"Yes" she whispered. Just before she came into my arms and her lips met mine.

"I'm feeling left out here guys." Said Lucy.

"And your point?" said Renée.

This time I was the one that started to laugh. Soon all three of us were laughing quite hard. Despite all the kissing and hugging we went back to work putting together the robot body. By 6 p.m. we had completely assembled a model 2 robot. All that was lacking was the CPU and programming to make it move.

Lucy said, "You know, it would be great if we glued that dildo copy of Jim's cock right here." She was pointing at the pelvis area of the model 2 robot. Just before she started giggling again.

"Oh Lucy" said Renée.

"Well it looks to me like you'll get the real thing shortly" said Lucy.

The telephone rang, and I answered it. It was dad he wanted to tell me that I was on my own for supper. He had a job that he needed to get done before he could come home, mom was working until midnight and my brothers and sisters were over at Grandma's house. After hanging up I explained to the girls what the phone call was about. Then I asked them what they want to do about it. Neither one of them seem to have any idea. But soon both were on their phones checking with her parents. As it turned out, both could get away for the evening.

I suggested that we try the new drive-in. It was called Don's and Millie's and they even had the waitresses on roller skates. Both of them agreed readily and soon we were piled in my car heading that way. The drive-in was full of cars mainly our fellow high school students but there were a few families there. Even Danny and Ben were parked across from us. And that resulted in a little harassment on the part of my best friends.

"So does this mean you're taking Renée to the prom?" Asked Ben.

Renée said, "Yes it does."

To which I got strange looks from the two of them.

Danny said, "The rest of this year is going to be really boring."

I started to laugh and so did Ben. Soon all of us were laughing. We ended up having a good time until Danny try to put his arm around Lucy. What happened next look like a scene from a kung-Fu movie. Lucy had twisted Danny's arm up around up behind him. She grabbed his fingers on the other hand bent them back and lifted them up above his head. Then she walked Danny back to his car.

"It's time you learned to ask before you make a move on somebody." Lucy said in a stern voice.

You could almost see the tears in Danny's eyes from the treatment. He squeaked out a weak okay in response. Lucy returned to my side took my left arm and put it around her. Renée tucked herself in under my right arm. And I was so confused I did know what to think of this. Renée kissed my cheek and whispered in my ear "I told you we share everything."

I think that the light finally went on in my little brain. These two have become such good friends that there was no way they would ever become separated.

Ben said, "Wow, you are one lucky dude Tim."

I grinned sheepishly at this news. After a little while we were finished eating Danny had left in a huff but Ben said he could get a ride from here so we returned to my house, and tried to decide what our next steps were going to be to build this android.

I said, "I guess we'd better order the rest of the stuff we need."

The two of them agreed. And soon we are gathered around my computer. Renée suggested that we get the molds ordered first. It didn't take long and my debit account was drained. Renée produced her card from her purse. And soon we got everything ordered. And the transactions were complete. Lucy needed to use the restroom. When she entered the room we herd "oh wow." It was plain to me that she was seeing the Jacuzzi bathtub.

Renée then called up a web site and computer. It was one that her father had suggested that had to do with artificial muscles. It was basically an elastic rubbery material that expanded and contracted in response to positive or negative electronic charges. In other words a positive charge caused the material to expand and a negative charge caused it to contract. I started absent-mindedly rubbing Renée's back as she read aloud what was on the screen. When Renée was done reading she explained that if this material is cut into muscle shapes and attached to plastic leg bones as are found in the human body then, with the right wiring and computer program we would be a lot closer to making a real android rather than just a robot. I had to agree, heck I did not even know things like this were out there.

Next Renée called up another medical site. This one had to do with artificial skin that was being used to replace burn victim's natural skin. I was enthralled with the information and didn't notice that Lucy was scratching my back. Renée turned to look at me and saw what Lucy was doing and she smiled. That's when I realized that Lucy was naked. Lucy looked at me and asks, "You think we could try your Jacuzzi?"

What could I say but "yes," and soon the three of us were naked in the Jacuzzi enjoying the hot bubbly water. Our talk continued about the possibilities of building a real android based on the new information we get. The girls had gathered one at each side and pressed their naked bodies close up to me.

Lucy asked, "Tim, like do you ever play with yourself in here?"

I turned slightly red. When Renée said, "well if he doesn't I'm going to."

With that I felt Renée hand wraparound my cock. Then she kissed me.

"Then what about me?" said Lucy.

So I put my around her and pulled her in for a kiss as well. It was a long kiss and lot of tongue was involved. Renée continue to play with my cock as Lucy's hand started to rub over my chest. Between the two of them I was getting quite excited. I pulled them both closer to me running my hands down their backs and squeezing their butts. Both of them let out low moans at my touch. This encouraged me and soon my fingers were on their way and very pleasantly feeling woman flesh. I continue to rub my fingers over the knobs that I found between their legs. Both girls let out low moans in response. I figured I was doing something right. Lucy's hand then found its way down to my cock as well. She started rubbing it in step with Renée's hand. Her head found its way to my chest where she started to suckle and lick what she found there. When Renée broke her current kiss with me her head dropped and she started on the other side doing the same thing.

It didn't take long for way too much stimulation and soon globs of white goop floated around the water. The girls continued as if nothing happened and I briefly wondered if either one of them had been with the boy before. I mean they were doing everything perfect but what they were doing seemed more like what they would do to each other than to a guy. Then I remembered a remark one of them made about a strap on dildo. Both girls were panting now and had moved my thumbs deep inside themselves as my fingers worked on their clitorises. I was quickly rewarded with moans of ecstasy from the two of them. Both had stopped doing anything to me as I worked on their love folds with my fingers. I also realize that, despite the fact, I had come, I was still hard as a rock.

Finally I asked the question that was on my mind. I said, "Tell me have either one of you ever actually done it before? I mean like with a boy."

Renée said in whisper, "no, you'll be my first."

Lucy said, "as long as I can be your second I'll let you be my first, maybe even my last."

Let me tell you words like 'you can be my first and my last' have a powerful effect on the male ego and I was no exception. I lifted René with one hand (it is easy to do in the water) until she was on top of me then whispered, "you want to do it here or should we go to the bed? Renée said let's try the bed first. And that's what we did.

I would like to have carried her unfortunately my stomach was still too sore. The smile the two of them gave me made up for it. Soon our wet bodies made their way to my bed and Renée lay on her back, legs high in the air. Her hand guided me between her legs, then gently took hold of me and guided my cock into her heavenly place. I pressed gently into her slowly, moving an inch at a time until I was completely buried inside of her. Lucy's hands started roaming our bodies as she tried to help us. Renée squeezed my hips with her legs; she was encouraging me to move and I started to move in and out of her, slowly at first as she was so tight, so wet and felt so good ... In a few moments I was worried about setting a new land speed record. Lucy had settled in next to Renée, her mouth finding the nipple of her breast and I could see her tongue reaching out as it flicked across it. The sight was too erotic for me and I came hard. I was deep inside of her as the floodgates opened and my seed filled her up. It was like nothing I had ever felt before. In that moment I saw more fireworks then I knew existed and I also understood that every dream I ever had was fulfilled with this one moment in Renée.

I was exhausted, and I was sore when I rolled off her. Only to be shocked again when Lucy move her face between Renée's legs. I couldn't believe what I was seeing. I mean it was like seeing a porn flick right off the Internet. I muttered "Unbelievable" to which Renée smiled at me and whispered, "I love you."

I said, "I love you too."

She pulled my face into her lips and kissed me deeply. I kissed her lips and up to her nose then down to her neck tell I was finely licking at her nipple. She let out a deep moan that means I think she came. And gently her hand nudged my head towards her left breast and I inhaled it into my mouth. My tongue lashed out across her nipple and her groaning grew until she seemed to explode. Her screech of pleasure made me happy no one was home. Soon however she seemed to be overwhelmed and her hand gently pulled my head away. Her other hand did likewise to Lucy and soon Renée lay in a foetal position mumbling about it being too much.

That's when I felt Lucy's warm lips around my Dick. Talk about a surprise it wasn't even hard when she started to suck but the warmth of her mouth and the feel of her tongue across the bottom of my manhood soon had it at its biggest ever. I was lying on my back with Renée tucked into my chest when Lucy said, "my turn", as she climbed up on top of me. Soon, as if in a dream, I felt the length of my shaft sliding into the second light of my life. Oh shit I thought, I wonder if I'm going to live through this. Lucy started to ride me like a cowgirl on a bucking bronco. She sure seems to know what she was doing and she proved to be just as noisy as Renée. It didn't take me long to come despite the fact that it was my third time that evening and Lucy was right behind me. As she finished she fell forward on top of me. If she hadn't been breathing so hard I would have been worried but after a few moments I realized she had passed out. At the same time Renée started to kiss me again. She started to mumble I love you between kisses mixed with a few thank-you thrown in as well.

It must've been too much for me as I too fell asleep. I didn't wake up until I heard feet traipsing across the floor as they entered the front door. The family was home dad must picked everybody up after he finished working.

"Oh shit, I said.

With that both of the girls were wide-awake and looked quite panicked about our predicament.

"Hush, hush I said. They're up stairs, we're down here and they don't normally come down."

They both giggled a little. Then we started to dress. Fortunately we were completely dressed before we heard the footsteps coming downstairs. It was my dad and he called out, "how are you coming down here Tim?" as I stepped out of my room with both girls in tow.

"Okay" I said.

"So how's the robot android thingy coming?"

"Pretty good said Renée as they had reached the bottom of the stairs. He looked over the model 2 that was completely assembled now. Then he had a strange look in his face. Oh crap I thought he could smell the odour of our sex. But he didn't say anything about it. Instead he went over inspected the robot more closely.

We ended up talking about the project for over an hour. When we heard mom come home we realized how late it was. Then both the girls excused themselves saying that they had to get home as it was after their curfew. Dad suggested that they call home before they leave and let their folks know that they had just lost track of time working on the project. Both girls agreed and were soon on their cell phones again.

Renée's parents were not upset at all. They just told her to hurry along, as, with a school day tomorrow, she needed to get plenty of sleep. Lucy's father however did not answer his phone and that caused Lucy to become concerned. I suggested that maybe I should go with her to make sure everything was OK. She agreed and Renée called her father back and told him what was going on. Shortly after that we showed up at Lucy's house. It was dark as if no one was home and her father's car was not in the driveway. We entered her house and everything was fine. She found a note from her father on the refrigerator. It stated that he had to go to Chicago on short notice and that if she didn't want to stay at home alone she should see if she could stay at Renée's.

Once the mystery was solved. The two girls went to Renée's house and I returned home. Of course when I kissed them goodnight both of them wished me a happy birthday. Then giggled as they left. Well, I thought, if that wasn't the best birthday present I have ever received.

When I arrived dad was waiting and we ended up having a long talk. Somehow I think he should have had the talk about the birds and the bees a long time ago. His timing wasn't always the best but in the end his advice turned out to be - if I was going to continue a relationship that involves sex with those two girls, either one or both of them, I should get the shot. Or, in his opinion, we all should go get the shot. I can't say I disagree with him as I knew I was not ready to become a father yet.

That night my dreams were filled with thoughts of two girls with big bellies. When I awoke that morning I decided that did not sound like a good idea and I would have to check with the school nurse sometime today. I would also have to make mention of this possibility to the girls at lunch.

Wednesday

I pulled into the parking lot by the school and found two girls waiting for me to arrive. They were both very excited see me for some reason and I received two very wet kisses. What a way to start your school day I thought.

As we were walking into the school I mentioned that I was going to go to see the school nurse about getting the shot and the two girls giggled and said "oh, now the boy thinks of it, it's a good thing we thought of it yesterday". It seemed the two of them had already been to the school nurse and got their shots. Well I guess that only leaves me. I think I will take dads advice just to be on the safe side. After we entered the school. We went our separate ways until lunchtime.

I was shocked when I entered my second hour study hall. You guessed it we had a substitute none other than Mrs. Clare Rumbskin. Somehow I just knew this was going to be a problem. Mrs. Rumbskin locked her evil eyes on me the moment I stepped in the room. I looked away from my seat and started to finish my homework from the day before.

Mrs. Rumbskin walked over in front of me and said, "I said that there'll be none of that young man."

To which I said, "Pardon?"

"I warned you young man. I'm not putting up with any of your backtalk."

"I don't understand?"

"That does it young man, to the office with you."

"What did I do?"

To which Mrs. Rumbskin reached out and grabbed me by the ear, and pulled me out of my seat.

"Hey, watch it, I'm still not recovered," I protested.

But she ignored me at she proceeded to pull me out of the room. Fortunately I did not hit my head on the way out. We didn't make it very far when the new officer intercepted us.

"What's going on here?" He asked. "This young man was being a disruptive influence on the class and when I told him to quit he became belligerent with me."

"As that so?" The officer asked.

"No sir" I said. To which she twisted on my ear harder. My discomfort was instantly obvious to the officer.

"That'll be enough of that! Release that young man now."

"But he'll get away." she protested.

"Do it now!" he ordered.

She then released my ear, which I instantly grabbed in order to further protect it. I moved up against the wall away from her and she screamed, "See he is getting away".

As she started to pursue me the school officer stepped between the two of us and said, "That'll be enough of that. I think we better take this to the office."

Mrs. Rumbskin complained the whole way there and told the cop what a bad individual I was. I keep my mouth shut all the way and as we entered the office the Secretary rolled her eyes into the top of her head and motioned for us to enter the principal's office.

The superintendent was sitting behind the desk and he just moaned when he saw the three of us. Mrs. Rumbskin immediately started to babble her rhetoric but the superintendent held up his hands stop her. Then he pointed to the officer and ask them to tell him what he knew. Mrs. Rumbskin became belligerent at his tone and the superintendent asked her to leave the room until he was ready for her. She arrogantly left the room and the superintendent asked the officer to continue his story. The officer explained what he is observed. Then he asked me what had happened. And after I completed telling him he apologized to me much to the surprise of the officer. Then he had to explain to the officer what he thought the problem really was. It looked to me like the officer was doing all he could to control himself and keep from laughing. Then the superintendent asked the officer if he would kindly watch over our study hall, until he could send a replacement. The officer agreed and we left the office towards my study hall. As we left he called Mrs. Rumbskin into his office. We could hear her yelling all the way back to the study hall.

I never did find out the results of her tirade, all I know is I never saw her again. The remainder of my class was uneventful as it only lasted 10 minutes after our return and the officer never did get relieved.

Science class consisted of yet another lecture but we were allowed the last half of class to work on our projects.

Chapter 10

Before class was over our teacher came over to talk to us some more. It seems that she was quite impressed with our proposal. And she was feeling guilty that we really didn't have enough time to properly complete this project. We explain to her that we thought we could get the basic structure of the android put together on time. To which she wished us luck and offer does any and assistance we could use. That's when Renée asked if Lucy could be part of our team. Lucy was taking the same class just a different hour. Strangely art teacher agreed despite the fact that it would leave her partner on his own. But she did they could be much of a problem. Because the two of them weren't getting along that well. Unbeknownst to me she had partnered with Danny. In the end she said we talked to Lucy and it sure was okay with her and see what you can arrange.

Lunchtime

Lucy, Renée and I seated ourselves to a nice fried chicken lunch. We herd the ruckus over at the table with Danny and Ben. I was kind of shocked as Ben didn't normally argue with anybody. Ben however looked like he had enough. And he picked up a tray and walked away. He looked over at us and I smiled at him. To which he walked up and asked very politely if he could join us. I motioned him to sit down and asked, "So what was that all about? What can I say I was curios? "Oh he said Danny is upset because I don't want to be his partner for the science project. It seems that Lucy is getting reassigned. And my other partners are as clueless as he is. The three of us just grinned at him.

"Oh, so you already know" he said.

"Yes" I said, "I was there when Renée suggested it."

Lucy said, "Yes I needed to thank you two for that."

Ben then said, "Well I told Bozo he could have my partners. Danny just doesn't know the first thing about robots."

"Oh, what exactly is you're class project Ben?"

"Were supposed to build an android, But Jim Peterson hasn't got the vaguest idea how to do it. Renée then said, "Hay, that's are project maybe Jim and Danny would be perfect for each other."

The girls started to giggle and soon Ben I started to chuckle. Well it sounded like a good idea anyways. We spotted our science teacher entering the cafeteria. And waved her over to our table. We then explain their idea to her, and she thought it would be a good idea. She said that she had been meaning to mention that other kids in other classes at the same types of assignments and was okay to collaborate with each other. After she left the table thought for us started to compare notes.

As it turns out and had not gotten as far as we had with the project. He was intrigued with the approach we were taking. Before lunch was over it was decided that the four of us would meet at my place to work on the android tomorrow night.

Basically the rest of the day was boring. The girls already had other plans for the evening so it looked like I was on my own. After I got home I spent several hours surfing the net for some of the advanced ideas we had already discussed. I was becoming very fascinated by all the possibilities that were actually out there.

Ben apparently had the same idea is me. And I wasn't too surprised when he IM to me. I sent him the links, especially the one on joint replacement that Renée's dad had provided to us. We chatted back and forth for a few hours as each of us searched the net. I found out, Ben's father had access to one of the new plastic modeling computer systems. The system basically takes a CAD design and using lasers produces a hard plastic model. This ended up in another search where we discovered that CAD designs were available online from the local medical University. Ben down loaded all of them. We also discovered that CAD designs for every organ in the human body including the muscle system also existed. Soon we had more information than we thought possible. Ben was going to check with his father to see if he could get plastic models of all the bones in the human body. Renée and Lucy signed on from Renée's house and we shared all the information we had found with them.

That's when Renée dropped a bombshell on us. Her father had made arrangements for the three of us to talk to a professor up at the University. It seems that the professor had some grant money on a proposal to produce a better skin for burn victims. And the professor was very interested in the possible application of this skin to androids. The meeting was set up for one week from Saturday.

I collapsed in bed that night. And of course ended up having dreams of two pregnant androids strangely they looked just like Renée and Lucy.

Thursday.

School was once again boring. And nothing really happened before we were done with the day. Except of course for four of us gathered for launch and talk things over.

That evening we all met at my house. And the conversation quickly turned to the adult doll site. Lucy took Ben over to my computer to show him. Leavening me and Renée time to kiss and hug. At least most of the soreness was gone for my stomach now.

When Lucy and Ben came out of my room. Ben been surprised me by asking if we were serious about forming a company. Renée indicated that yes we were. And Lucy was bouncing around the room.

Renée whispered in my ear that she thought Lucy really liked Ben. I whispered back that it was no surprise to me he was such a likable guy. I got another long kiss for my comment.

Renée and I snuggled up on a couch. Where we were necking and just generally making out. When we noticed the two of them holding hands as they lifted the canvas cover off the painting. The look on Bens face was priceless and left him speechless unlike Lucy who started chatting a mile a minute about how wonderful the painting was. After Ben recovered from his shock he plainly stole glances at Renee. Lucy noted it and must have had a moment of inspiration. She asks me if I could do a painting of her as well. What could I say, "Yes, after we get the project done."

Renee whispered in my ear, "I think Ben might want to become a partner." I grinned thinking about how fast we could actually build the units with four of us working on them.

That's when Ben asks us the question.

"You know, if we incorporated the business right now. We could force the ownership of all R&D to the company and avoid any potential problems with the school system in the future." Ok it was more of a statement then a question.

I had to ask, "Why do you think the school system would be a problem in the future?"

"Well once the project is entered in the science fair competition, the intellectual rights to the project pass to the school system. They do it that way to keep the kids from being ripped off by others. But the real reason is the royalties some company will have to pay to the school system."

Lucy exclaimed, "Hay that's not fair."

Renee said, "How do we stop it from happening?"

Ben grinned, "By incorporating a business now, and making the intellectual rights the property of the company."

"I don't get it. How will that stop the school system from claiming they have royalty rights?"

"Simple, they will be unwilling to sign any paper that says they have to pay royalties to the company."

Lucy asked, "So then the project wouldn't be shown at the science fair?"

"Yes, it will be shown, well the prototype one will be shown. However the school will not be able to negotiate with companies to sell the rights for use. The company with the rights will be able to dictate the rights are not for sale."

I grind with the realization of what he was saying. The school system would not be able to sell the rights to use are science project to a third party. Are business would already own the rights, so we wouldn't have to pay the school system a dime. And best of all, we would already have a business started. I liked the sounds of it.

Renee asks, "Ben, how do you know all this legal stuff?"

"Because my ex step mom was the school systems attorney and I remember her talking about how the system was taking advantage of compulsory education to fatten the systems pocket books."

"So how many times has the school system actually even made money off science projects?"

"Two or three times in the last 10 years that I can think of."

"Wow, that's a lot more then I would have expected" I said.

"But won't incorporating be expensive?"

"Nope, my step Mom will do it for free. She loves me."

I started to crack up. Ben was right behind me in his laughter. It was at the expense of the girls. But you would never get either one of us to tell the girls why.

Renee and Lucy looked at us expectantly. Finally they ask in unison, "What so funny?"

I just pointed to Ben and he tried to shake off the question. The girls would have none of that. Finally he said, "Let's just say she gave me privet lesions in how to treat a woman."

Renee let out a gleeful laughed when she relished what Ben had said. Lucy on the other hand just said, "Your own Mother?"

"Step Mother."

"That still doesn't sound right."

"Oh, Girls please, don't tell anyone." Ben asks with the sudden realization that they now knew his secret.

"I think it's cute." Renee said.

"It still doesn't sound right to me."

"Lucy I said. "She was closer to Ben in age then she was to Ben's Father."

Lucy seemed to puzzle over it a few moments. Then the realization hit her that Ben had experience in the form of training. So she said, "Ok I won't tell anyone, but the training she gave you better have been worth it." Then she looked him in the eye with a mischief's grin on her face.

Ben Gulped but recover and said, "Well, you'll just have to judge for yourself." Then he made his Gaucho Marx eyes at her. Lucy and Renee started to giggle.

I decided it was time to change the subject. So I said, "Well here is an important question then."

The giggles died down and everyone looked at me. So I continued. "Do the four of us what to go into the sex android business together?" Then I looked at Renee. She nodded yes and looked to Lucy. Lucy said, "Yes." And all eyes turned to Ben. He said, "I wouldn't miss it for anything." Then everyone looked at me. What could I say? So I said, "Ok then we are in agreement, Ben call your Step Mom."

"Ok" he said and took out his cell phone. He of course had the number on speed dial and his step mom Alice answered on the 4th ring. He explained that the four of us had a business idea and wanted her to do an incorporation before we submitted the science project in 5 weeks. We all had to get on the phone and give her are personal information. For some reason it took 4 corporate offices to make up a company. The hard question, who was going to hold what office and how much stock the company was going to have. In the end we decided that we would have to decide this and get back to her. She also said we need to make up a business plan. This idea was getting more complicated by the minuet. When Alice relished we need to be walked thought the process she set up an appointment for the four of us at her office on Saturday. It was a good thing, as the phone call resulted in more questions than answers.

After Ben hung up, the 4 of us sat down to go over things. It was decided that Ben would be the corporate president, I would be Vice President, Renee would be the treasure and Lucy would be the secretary. Once we came to a decision, we realized we were not getting any work done on the android. So the discussion turned to what we had, what we could do for the school project and what we thought we could do with the company. Ben said that we should wait until Saturday and get his stepmothers advice on the finances before we went any father with spending the money on materials. We were all in agreement, but we took the time to modify the project plan for school. Are planed date for casting Renee's body would be on Sunday? From that we could make the plaster model and make the die to place around the android. We also decided that the android need to more then walk. Since the routine to walk a model 2 was simple. We decided we needed to make the android talk as well. Lucy was the one that understood animatronics. She said that if Ben could code things, she could come up with the unit to make the androids mouth move.

Ben and Lucy left around 8 that evening. Renee and I were enjoying the piece and quite now that they had left. We held on to each other and petted as we kissed until she had to go home at 930. I was actually hurting after she left. Too much stimulation and no release had given me blue balls. Oh well, tonight I would just have to reintroduce Mr. Johnson to rosy Mary.

Friday.

School was finally back to normal. My teachers seemed to be back to normal around me. I guess the novelty of what happened wore off. At least they are not looking at me funny anymore.

Science class was odd today. Are teacher looked at us kind of funny after she read the project plan updates. That's when it hit me that we had listed the meeting with the attorney on Saturdays as part of the progression. Perhaps she was worried about an attorney getting involved. She didn't say anything however and the day went by normally. Until lunch time that is.

Danny was in rare form again. Let's see what would be the best way of putting it. He was acting like a younger sibling, making kiss faces and the like around the four of us. I think he was jealous that we were not sitting with him. He instead was sitting with the confirmed stoners. The pot heads that is.

The day was finely over and of all things I found myself alone for a change. Lucy and Renee had Monica's birthday party that night. No guys allowed for some reason. Ben was going to work on his computer routines. He really was a nerd when it came to computers. It was good thing for him he didn't look like one. As for me, well I decided after my homework was done to get on line.

I search the Internet even more closely for stuff on androids. It's odd to think about it like this, but I figured my mind was already putting together a 2nd generation unit and I was already thinking on the third. What I mean by that is the first generation would be life like silicon over a robotic frame. The second generation would also be a sex bot but the frame would be semi based on a human circulative system and prosthetic muscle tissue. And the third generation would be synthetic skin. The big issue that still needed to be crossed was an AI brain. As I searched deeper on the net, I found a professor at Berkley had come close to AI. His progress was limited however, it seems the computer AI would begin to auto program itself and then erase itself for some reason. There were many theories as to way. I think my favorite was that it realized it was not human, could never be human and there for calculated it would be best not to be. In other words, it committed suicide.

Chapter 11

Casting day.

Renee showed up at 9am ready to begin. Wellbeing novice to begin would be more like it. Lucy showed up 15 minutes later and Ben called to apologies because he forgot he had to go to his Great Aunt Millie's birthday party at noon. He said he would be over as soon as he could get away but we should start without him.

I had a table set up for us to work on. It was moms old massage table out of the garage so it wasn't as high as I would have liked. However it would take the weight without a problem. I explained that we would make a total of 7 casting of her body in four stages.

Renee asks, "What does that mean?"

"Well we will make one casings each of her legs at the same time. Then we would do the same for her arms. Her torso would be next and finally your head."

"Oh."

Lucy chimed in, "Hay what about her hair?"

Renee looked at me as if in dread. I knew why as well. She had shaved all the hair from her body below her neck. Fortunately I had it covered. I went over to the work bench and held up a bathing cap. Renee looked relived.

"So what do we do after we have all the castings of her body?" Lucy asks.

"Simple, we then pour in plaster of Paris and make the master mold."

"So why not just make the mold of her body from the main casting?"

"Well, it would be very difficult to do that. Besides, I can work on the master casting and make a perfect mold. You see I not only have to play sculpture on the plaster model, I have to shave the head area down to the proper scull size. I will also be able to get rid of any imperfection that happen from when we make the casting.

"Oh" the girls said in unison.

With that is was tame too start the molding process. So I said, "Renee time to get in that natural state I like to see you in. She blushes slightly but shed her clothing. Soon we had Renee on the massage table and I got out the bottle of baby oil. I said we can skip this step when we get around to doing Lucy's casting." To which I got a playful slap from Lucy and, "I am really sorry about that. I hope you will forgive me some day."

What could I say? Well how about, "Well if you get in the same state as Renee is. It will go a long way towards that."

"You just want me naked as well."

My smile gave away my true intent.

Renee said, "I think I would be more comfortable if we were all naked. Besides it will be just like summer vacation anyway."

Lucy was laughing and it was contagious.

"I surrender," I said, as I pealed out of my clothing. Well at least we were all naked. I noted with some satisfaction that Lucy had also removed her hair from her body below the neck.

"Nice shave job." I muttered as I went back to oiling up Renee.

"Oh no razors."

"What?" I asked.

Renee said, "We used that cold wax stuff."

"You waxed?"

Lucy, "Yes, and we already decided we are going to keep using the stuff until we never have to shave or wax again."

"Really, sound like it would be painful."

"Oh not at all. Well there was some at first. Until we learned that you had to pull really fast."

"Oh." Was all that came out of my mouth?

Soon we were pouring liquid latex over Renee's legs. She was complaining about having to keep then lifted up. Then I helped her to sit up and hang her leg over the edge of the table. It only took 10 minutes from the first coat to the last of the latex. It looked thick enough to me. It would be cured up enough to remove in another 10 minutes.

It was when I went to remove the latex from her legs we discovered the first problem. Suction keeps me from pulling them off.

"Now what do we do?" Renee asked.

"Simple, we amputate." I said as I picked up a small knife.

"You aren't really going to cut her legs off?" Lucy looked in shock.

"Of course not. I am just going to put a hole in the bottom of the latex here at her foot. Renee looked wide-eyed at the knife. She was holding her breath as I poked a small hole between her toes. Then I started to pull on the latex again. This time it pulled away and slid down her well-oiled legs.

"Well that didn't hurt me."

"I would never want to hurt you my lovely little android." I wiggle my eyes like I was almost blinking. Renee laughed at my poor attempt at moving my eyebrows around.

"Hay that looked funny, but can you do it as you are kissing me?"

I kissed her and of course my dick was growing at the same time. I felt baby oil being squirted on my cock and looked at Lucy.

"We need a second copy of your cock for when you're not around." She said.

Well I guess she was right. They only had one. I surged and Renee grabbed my cock and started to rub it. "It will do in a pinch, but to tell the truth I like the real one better."

"My arms are getting tired now." Renee said after the first three minutes.

"I believe you, but you look so cute like that."

"Like what?"

"With your arms out to your side and your breast pointing at me like that. Beside Mr. Johnson likes what he sees."

Renee and Lucy looked down at my cock covered in latex and giggled. At least we remembered the baby oil this time.

After ten minutes I removed the castings from Renee's arms with Lucy's help. Actually Lucy and Renee were pulling at the latex on my cock. They were teasing me as I worked because they could have just let me shrink down without any attention. The thing would have fallen off in time.

Ben had just come bonding down the steps calling out, "I'm here to help. I heard I would get to see a naked..." He stopped dead in his track at the bottom of the steps. He was dumbfounded at the site before him. I mean here were to naked girls and myself. The girls playing with the latex on my cock. We looked at his face and started to laugh.

"Err Sorry, Um..."

"Knock it off Ben, Get used to it. You're going to be working around naked androids very soon anyway."

The girls were still giggling and Ben was still standing there with his jaw on the floor. He looked like he was ready to bolt. However before he could do just that. Lucy went over to him with a smirk on her face. You know the type of smirks that looked like a cat that just ate the canary looks. Ben was staring wide-eyed at Lucy's approach. His eye ready to pop out as she reached him. Lucy took Ben by the hand and led him into rec-room. As he was guided into the center of the room Ben was making small sound that no one could tell what they meant. I figured from the sounds it was just nervous mutterings myself. Renee spoke, "It was nice if Lucy and Mike to get naked with me. It took away some of the building tension I had. She said batting her eyelashes at him. PLOP the mold of my cock dropped to the floor. Before those red eyelash started the blood flowing in that area again. Everyone was looking down at it. The moment lingered no one was laughing but the tension was their ready to brake though the moment.

Renee spoke first, "Ben, you wouldn't mind making me feel comfortable too would you?"

"What?" Ben looked up at Renee sitting there before him on the table.

She giggled, "Your clothes"

"What" Ben sputtered, "What about my clothes?"

"Would you take them off please?"

Ben went rigid in disbelief. However Lucy started to pull his shit up over his head as she said, "Of course he will." Somehow Ben managed to lift his arms as his tee was pulled over his head.

"Oh goody" Renee said, "Maybe we can get a mold of his cock as well."

I couldn't take it anymore. I sat down hard on the table next to Renee and started to laugh my ass off. I mean I couldn't help myself. I was envisioning all that hair stuck to the latex. My laugher first brought looks of confusion even if Renee was smiling as she looked at me.

"What are you laughing at?" Ben asked.

"Your hair, I mean your hair trapped in the latex." He did have a vary hairy chest. Lucy was eyeing it as she undid Ben's jeans. Then she slid her hand though the hair on Ben's chest. Her fingers entwine though the hair as her hand moved to his left tit. Ben looked like he was going to blow a load in his pants at her touch. His cock was tenting out his boxers thou the open fly on his blue jeans. When Lucy said, "I think we can do something about that."

Ben was bewildered and asked "What?"

Lucy's smile was turned up full boar when she said, "The hair."

"What about the hair?"

"We will remove it, I don't really like it."

"Remove." Ben stuttered over the word.

"Yes, you will let me do that won't you? As she planted a kiss and a lick on his left tit."

"Ohhh..." Ben groaned.

"Is that a yes?" Lucy said as she licked again.

"Yes, anything for you." Ben blurted out. "Just don't stop doing that."

Lucy's hand then slid down Ben's front and into his briefs she was grabbing on to what she found there and spoke softly, "After the hair is gone, it tickles my nose and feel funny on my tong."

Mike's eyes almost crossed at the sensation on his cock. His body went rigid and a wet spot formed on the front of his boxers just before the motion of Lucy's had forced it though the opening in them. Ben cock then fired two more spurts into the air that unfortunately landed accost Renee and me.

"Oh my god." Ben said as is mind came back into focus. "That was incredible."

"Yes" I agreed "And messy as well." I was looking over at the cum that landed on Renee's stomach and my lap as I said this.

Ben seen where I was looking and said, "Oh sorry I couldn't help it. Really I couldn't."

I cut him off, "Yes these two have that effect on me as well. Trust me I have learned that about these little vixens."

Renee stuck out her tong at me but Lucy just pushed Ben's pants down the rest of the way. Saying, "Now it's time to clean him up." With that she started to lick the head of Bens cock off. Ben was only 7 inches long but only after a few licks his cock looked like it was going to grow to 8.

I don't think she had actually ever given a guy a blowjob before. Ben made a funny face a few times; I think she must have got him with her teeth. Renee was licking Ben's seed from my lap when her tong found my dick and from there I was the one in heaven. I closed my eyes enjoying the feeling on my manhood as her mouth enveloped me. She was moving slowly up and down almost tentatively as she went. I never felt her teeth but she was going slowly as she figure out how to do it. My mind was so on the feelings I was receiving I missed the action between Lucy and Ben. When I came it was like a volcano of hot lava flowing out the end. Renee turned into a suction cup and every drop went into her mouth. I finally opened my eyes and looked down at the smiling face in my lap.

She spoke, "Next time, no baby oil."

'Oh I had forgotten about that.'

There was a gasp at the bottom of the steps and everyone head turn in time to see my baby sister running back up the steps. There on the floor behind her was the basket of laundry she had been bringing down. My sister Debbie is only 11 and normally didn't ever come down stirs. Laundry was something that was sent down the chute in the bathroom.

"Oh shit." I said.

"Well she just got an eye full." Lucy spoke.

The three of them started their giggles and laughter at the situation. I just knew this was going to be a problem in the making. The four of us got cleaned up and just as the first coat of latex was being poured on Renee's front. My mom called down the stairs.

"Tim is someone naked down there."

"Yes, Mom we are making a casting of Renee's body today, remember?"

Mom was quite for a moment then said, "So why is everyone naked then?"

Gulp was my first reaction.

Renee, "It's only fair to me, I didn't want to be naked alone."

"I see, well no I don't approve. I think this needs to change right now. And you girls need to go home."

Shit, there was no way Renee could go any ware. We were still putting liquid latex on her to make a mold.

"It will be a few moments for the mold to set up mom. Besides dad gave his permission to do this."

"Your father never gave permission for you to have an orgy in the basement."

"Mom we are not having an orgy."

"If your friend are not out of this house in one..."

"What's going on?" my dad's voice could be herd over my moms. Then we could her them arguing. Then dad spoke up, "No orgies in the basement Tim, And how long before you're done?"

"Maybe two hours yet dad."

"See, I told you they were working down there. Two more hours for an orgy god I wish I could last that long. I know they can't."

My mom's voice could be herd but not what she was saying.

"Tim, I am going to take you mother, sisters and brothers out for a while. Your poor mother is beside herself over thus issue. Seems that Debbie is telling tall tales again."

"Okay Dad."

"Is two hours enough?"

"We will be done casting Renee by then. But we still have lots of other work to do here."

"I see, well everyone be dressed when we get back in two hours. I will come down there then and see if your mom's fears are founded."

"Gee whiz dad, you can come down now if you want." I put in and Ben went white as the girls giggled quietly.

"No, I don't need to see that." Mom's voice spoke, "You afraid Debbie is telling the truth?"

"No, I just don't think we have any right interfering with an 18 year olds love life."

"But it's my house, it should be my rules."

"Our house and my rules!" Dad said.

Mom could be herd cussing and well she stomped off.

"Tim she will come down. Meanwhile I think we all need to sit down and talk later."

With that dad and mom were gone.

"You going to be in trouble over this?" Renee asked me.

"Nothing my mom, we all are going to be in trouble."

Ben said, "Knowing his Dad, We will be ok though."

I chuckled a bit. How many times had Ben Danny and I getting into mischief only to have dad fix things after words. Dad always believe in letting boys be boys. Heck he was the one that helped create the model rocket fiasco. Don't ask, we should have never let him use copper pipe for the engine. It melted and crashed into the neighbor's roof. The fire really wasn't that bad. The insurance covered everything and well Mr. Donaldson next door was the one that pointed out that we should use steel pipe next time. I thought Mom was going to divorce dad after that. She had been so mortified. Actually I say mom is a traditionalist most of the time. The rest I think she lives in fear of what others think of her.

The four of us had finished the mold of Renee and had just poured the plaster in the molds to set up. It would be a few days before I could put the pieces together and make a proper modeling mold to work with. We had all gotten dressed and there hadn't been any hanky panky. Well unless you count the orgasm Renee had as my fingers found their way into her hole. I mean I was removing the mold and well they just ended up sliding inside her somehow.

Mom and dad came home and shortly they were coming down the steps. That's when the four of us saw Renee's parents and Ben's as well following behind her. Mom started,

"I just want everyone to know what is really going on here."

"What's that Dear?" My dad said.

"This is about sex."

"What's wrong with that Renee's dad asked?

"They are too young to be having sex?"

Dad said, "I seem to remember you started when you were 16."

"That's not the point."

Ben's Mom said, "I am confused."

"These four were having an orgy in the basement here." She spread her arms around make a point of the massage table. I guess the robot parts and plaster casting was what everyone seen.

"Looks like they have been working on their science project to me." Renee's mom said. "Are you sure they had time for an orgy?"

I was looking at Ben's step mom Carroll something or other. She was about 19 years old herself. God Ben's dad like them young. She was showing more skin then Renee and Lucy were at the moment. Ben's dad looked like he was proud to hear his son was involved in an orgy. Dad just looked perplexed, manly with mom and poor Renee's parents just plain looked confused.

Dad spoke, "This has gone far enough, Tim were you four having an orgy down here? Yes or no."

"No dad, no orgy."

"But they were all nude, that's what Debbie said."

Renee's dad, "That doesn't mean they were having an orgy. And even if they were their all 18 now I think?"

Ben raised his hand and said, "Next month."

"Close enough" Renee's dad said.

"Aren't you upset you daughter is have sex?" Mom piped in.

Renee's mom said, "Well to tell the truth, I am relived if she is having sex with a boy."

"What?"

"I said I am"

"No about boys?"

"Oh, well we have been kind of concerned about her dating. She hasn't shown an interest in boys before now."

"Well good for her but that's not why I ask you here."

Dad said, "And why did you ask them here?"

"I don't want orgies going on in my house!"

Everyone was staring at my mom. I mean what can I say, I guess that she was a bit on the prudish side.

"So" Ben's dad said, "You asked us over here to do what exactly?"

"I wanted you to support me on this issue."

Everyone looked at mom again. Then Renee's dad spoke, "Mrs. Miller, while I understand you don't want orgy's taking place in your house. Although I do not agree with there is anything wrong with orgies." His wife was smiling like the chasseur cat at this statement. "I believe we already determined there was no orgy taking place."

"Debbie say it and told me what she saw."

"And that was what ecstasy?"

"That everyone was naked and playing with each other."

"I see, so she didn't say they were fucking?"

Mom blushed, "No she said they were touching and kissing"

Dad said, "Of course they were touching Judy, they were making casting of Renee."

"That another thing, I don't like this project. Can't you do something else?"

"No mom, it's our assigned project."

"I still don't like all this sex stuff and technology stuff and I don't want it in my house."

Ben's dad asked, "So this is not about my son being involved in an orgy? I mean it's really only about a stupid school project?"

Dad considered it a moment. I don't think he really considered the school project as stupid. We really hadn't mentioned the business idea to any of the parents yet. However he answered,

"That would appear to be the case Mark." Mom was then giving him that look. The one she gave him just before he needed to find some ware to hide for a week. The one that said my way or the highway. Before she could explode however. Mark started to walk toward the stairs saying. "Well then, I don't think I need to be here. Come on Carroll, let's go see if we can find an orgy to attend." With that Carroll was in tow as they started to climb the stairs.

Mom was left speechless. Dad and the Rainer's were smiling and tiring very hard not to laugh. It didn't work when Ben couldn't hold it in and started too. Mom looked fit to be tied.

"Well if you don't put a stop to this affront before god then I will." With that mom left in a huff. No one was laughing after that.

Dad said, "Maybe it would be best if you worked on this project at someone else's house."

"Well Dad, I don't know were."

"You can use our guest house." Gloria Rainer chimed in. She was seconded a moment later by her husband.

"Well I don't know." I started to say but got a jab to my side from Renee and she said, "What a good idea."

"Do you know how many hours it will take me to work on just finishing the pre-mold?" I asked.

"Well the guest house has three bedrooms, so if you are working too late just spend the night."

"Mom!" Renee said.

Then her dad said, "Well if your mom objects too much. You can just move in there until you start collage."

Ok now my mouth was hanging on the ground. I don't think my dad could believe what he was hearing. Renee was beaming at the idea. Ben and Lucy had their eyes locked on each other. What do you bet we can both guess what the two were thinking about?

Somehow I managed an "Okay" and the next thing I know everyone is making plans to move me. Well I guess my Dad said it best. "Son, your mother can be a prude at times. This will teach her a good lesson."

Since it was close to time to meet with Bens Ex stepmother. It was decided that we would start moving the project stuff over after dinner.

My head was still swimming when we got to Linda's house. The meeting was very productive and informative. After all set into motion, I think the corporation idea made a lot of since. The four of us decided on the name Android-R-Us because for the most part they would be little more than sex toys. Despite being based on a model two frame.

Chapter 12

 Sunday ended up with me moving out of the house. I was very glad dad told me what he was going to do. He acted like he was taking mom's side and playing it up in the extreme. At first mom seemed pleased that dad had come around to her way of thinking. When he gave the ultimatum. I did my part and rejected it. This meant he was forced to though me out of the house. Mom did not like what was happening one bit. When she tried to protest me actually leaving, I mean it was like he is two young. How will he make a livening? Didn't you want him to work with you this summer? Well she sounded pitiful, so pitiful that I almost relented to her desires. Dad would have none of it though. He called a friend and by noon Sunday. There was a small moving van in the driveway. I really didn't have that much stuff. Well that's what I thought until the van was loaded. Bill and Eddy my little brothers were already arguing over my room down stairs. I had to remind them that whoever got it. The other would also get a room of their own.

Actually it was odd in a way. Once I was actually gone. Mom seemed to do a one eighty every other day. Dad now thinks she might be bi-polar. Ben says he doesn't see a difference in her. I guess when I was living with her I just didn't see it. One minute she would be a loving caring mother. There is nothing she wouldn't do for you. The next she wanted nothing to do with me. It was Renee and Lucy that pointed out that it really depended on if the girls were with me or not. As I thought about it I realized that if it was just me and her She acted loving. If it was me and Lucy she wanted to cut me out of the will.

It actually took the plaster a week to set up. It was the next Saturday that I actually started to put the casting together. I was glad dad intercepted mom from throwing the orders away as they arrived. Anyways it took me all day to fit everything together. Renee was by my side the whole time. When I had the plaster statue of her ready, smoothed and looking good. The Rainer's came over to look at it. I may have forgotten to mention that the Rainer house was clothing optional. That went for the guesthouse as well. So here us four are stark naked when Renee's parents walked in stark naked. It was a very weird feeling. But I was assured that I would get used to it. The Rainer's oh and ah the plaster of Paris statue. Ben had managed to modify the housing of the robot. Lucy had the animatronics of the mouth ready to go. It looked funny, but once the silicon would be place over it. Well we were going to be keeping our fingers crossed over it all working. Ben and Renee worked on the robots movement and speech routine. All the time we are working on the project every night and weekend. We keep coming up with new ideas.

When the day came to actually put the android inside the silicon. Ben showed up with the plastic bones his dad had gotten a friend to make for us. It was shortly after we got the silicon mixed with hardener poured in the mold. That the possibilities between the plastic bones, Artificial muscle and skin final took place in are mind.

When we talked over are idea of an anatomically correct non-mechanical body. We were shocked to learn it was already being done. Well not what we had in mind. There was a company that made fake cadavers for medical schools. This opened the door to us getting even more information on the human body. And more ideas for non-mechanical controls. They are more bioelectric. Only the bio part was not living real tissue. It was the fake stuff being developed for human replacement and prosthetics. Only the cadaver came close to what we were thinking of. The two weeks before the project was supposed to be presented. We got hold of some of the synthetic material intended for muscle replacement. It was experimental but since the government cut off the funding at the university hospital. The professor in charge of the program didn't have the funds to develop it anymore. So what did it end up costing us? Well, for the science project nothing. For the future of Androids he wanted 2% of the company's stock. Since we had decided on 1000 share and issuing each of us 240 with the other 40 shares going to out attorney for services and legal counsel. Somehow the 20 shares seemed like a fair price if we used his creation at all. When we voiced are concern, the good doctor sweetened the deal by offering us 10 hours a week of research time for a year. Are attorney suggested we jump on the offer. She was sure his time would be worth far more then he would be worth. I think she was thinking are company was going to be worth a few million. She would be proven wrong. As to how big it would get. Well you will just have to wait until we get to that part of the story.

We barely made the dead line with the submission of Amy the Android. Why Amy you ask. Well that is the name Renee wants to name her first girl someday. Besides it sounded better than the model 1 Android. Ben and Lucy had outdone themselves on the programming of Amy. The preplanned speech was 10 minutes in length. Of course it wasn't Amy that was the hold up. It was Frankie the arm. Yes Frankie for Frankenstein's monster. It was a collection of plastic arm bones that were covered with artificial muscle and the forearm was covered in synthetic skin donated by one of Dr. Tulane's research centers. It was meant for burn victims and had been infused with multiple micro sensors. As you looked at Frankie you had hand bones with noting on them. A wrist and arm covered in synthetic mussel and finely the skin started just above the elbow. We had it hooked up to Renee's dad's laptop. If we could have had more time, I think we could have gotten the arm to do more. As it was, Frankie was only meant to show the possible future development of the android we had envisioned.

We had Amy and Frankie set up in the Gym area with the rest of the schools projects. It was intended to be signal Saturday of display. Even of it took most kids a week to get theirs set up. We had taken a few hours on Friday to set up the table and backboard with the photo's I had taken of the process we used to make both Amy and Frankie. We covered them with blue sheets so no one could peek. I don't think any of the other kids would. But a few were looking around and their competition. Mainly the exhibits that were very large. One of these was on earthquakes. The Continental shift what the title on the banner behind it. Looked more like the 4 kids that worked on it had built a mini carnival ride. With all the hydraulic pumps under the platform.

Ben had used a simple RF remote control to let us control Amy. This meant with careful control, Amy could be used to carry Frankie in. Well that's how we got Frankie to the table Saturday morning. Amy just sat in the car seat. The girls had spent hours using die paints and pigments to give Amy a makeup. They even shaded the nipples and virgin the right colors. Not that anyone would see that. We had her in a simple black dress. The girls were surprised that Renee's dress fit so well. I just knew they were playing around with me. After all they were all their when we caste the molds. It was strange the wig they found. Because it was long and black it made Amy look more like that actress Char then Renee. Well I really didn't mind. We had a red wig at the guest house. When that one was on she looked just like my Renee.

I don't think Mr. Moray realized that Amy was not real. When she came in caring frank's arm. He asks if she was at the right high school. When the four of quit laughing we explained that she was are exhibit for the science fair. He then thought we were joking until Ben made her move with the remote.

Mr. Moray just said, "Well the rest of the attendees might as well go home."

He was probably right about who would win. Are teacher was going to be grading the assignments today. We were a bit nerviest about that. After all she never would actually answer are question about an AI brain. She would just tell us to do are best. She had seen all the plans and progress reports.

When the fair actually started everyone could look around but mostly the parents that came, only a few students showed up on a Saturday. I could understand that as none of us really wanted to be there on are day off either.

Are teacher finally got to are exhibit at 11. Since Amy was set up to be the star we started here presentation.

"Hello every one, my name is Amy." Pause. "I am the first fully functional robotic synthetic human look alike. That is to say I am the first generation android developed for this science project by Tim, Renee, Ben and Lucy the owners of androids r us Inc."

Our teachers face seemed to frown at that news. Before that she had been smiling widely at Amy's demonstration. Amy went on for the full ten minutes and explained everything about the process used in creating her and the future of android complete with a jerky wave from the Frankie arm. The audience was entranced by Amy even are teacher seemed to forget about the company name. When Amy finished her routine the question started. "Yes Amy was not only anatomically correct but fully functional. Well no she didn't eat or have to go to the bathroom like humans did. Yes we could make more of them. Not sure how much we would sell them for. That last question was from Lucy's dad of course. The questions went on and on. It was two o'clock when the fair was over. We were about to take down are exhibit when Are principle came over and ask us to leave it here until tomorrow at noon. When Mr. Rainer ask why, he said the news people would be her around ten and he wanted us to give a demonstration of Amy to the camera. He had been very impressive with the life like looks. Are teacher did give us an A for are project even if Amy really didn't have a brain in her head. I think it was Frankie that caused it though. Since he was so different than anything she had seen before. Well he was the future of robotics peoples and Ben had coined the phrase.

We celebrated that night at Baja's. Mr. Rainer took us all out for dinner. Dad even showed up to join us. Mom did not of course. She was still mad at me for leaving. Somehow she had convinced herself that it was all Renee's fault. She did not want to be around Renee ever again. Well that is what dad said anyways. Lucy's dad was there as was Ben's Dad and some girl named Marjory. Seems she was an exotic dancer, well that is what she said she was. We all know that means she was a striper. Our dinner went well and Dr. Rainer made his announcement that he was glad the law suit was over. It seems that the hospital had finally relished old man barns as part of the deal my lawyer worked out. So officially the hospital had paid the 5 million and the deal was done. I was dumb struck. He seemed confused.

"I don't understand, that is what your lawyer said it would take to end the law suit?"

Dad said, "But we don't know anything about this. We have never ... He paused. "Tim did you agree to this?"

"No dad, in fact I had forgotten all about it."

"I am going to guess it was your mother?"

"Well I guess that's your department." Personal I was trying to consider what to do with the 5 million dollars. Maybe my own place for real would be a good start. Then again are company could use a place to work out of.

Anyway the money was soon left behind as the discussion turned to tomorrow and the local news channel.

Saturday was fun as we demonstrated Amy and Frankie for the TV station. They were there an hour and a half and ask us far more questions than the crowd had the day before. Ho long until we could finish Frankie. Would it be a male or female? If Amy had been fully tested for function. Right I knew just what they were asking. When they got to who was the mold, Renee jumped in and said I was an artist and crated a sculpture to uses just for this.

The four of us sat around at the Rainer's watching the evening news that night. They ran a nice segment on Amy and Frankie even if it was less than 2 minutes long. Dad called me on my cell phone shortly after that. He had not seen the news, but Mom was gone. She isn't show up after work last night. When dad called to see if she was still at the hospital she hadn't been in to work at all. In fact no one had seen her since Saturday at noon.

Mom's disappearance was indeed a mystery. The police carefully explained that the odds were she had run off with another man. Dad was left at home with the hellions, as I liked to call my brothers and sisters. All was not sitting right in Denmark as the old saying goes.

Monday was a normal day at school. Well if you can call all the attention we got normal. There were a few nay Sayers. The stoner crowd with Danny in the lead. It wasn't all that bad in my opinion. However Ben went ballistic over the quality control joke. Or was it the one about the fried penis. Come to think of it I think it was one in the same joke.

I stopped by home after school to see the brats. I did miss not being around them. Dad was their home early from work. He called the lawyers office to find out if mom had something to do with the settlement. It came to us as a shock to find the line was disconnected. This led to other phone calls and finally a call to the officer handling moms missing person case. Let me tell you it was the next morning when the police were waiting to question me about mom that it was becoming apparent what had happened.

Mom and the lawyer had run off together with the 5 million dollars. It was that simple. My mother miss self-righteous and all stole my money and was probably living in sin with another man. Who would have thought it was possible? Not me and not dad that was for sure.

Will to make a long story short here. Only about mom. It seems the attorney paid her for a fool. The headed down though Mexico and ended up in Argentina. Where of all things mom was arrested on so many trumped up charges it wasn't funny. Not that I really cared what happened other than knowing for sure. I am sure she will have a fine life when she is extradited in 30 years or so. Seems Argentina doesn't what her if she lives though he sentence. The lawyer, well 5 million must go a lot farther down in Argentina than it does here. Because the Argentine government swore to us they can't find him. Funny thing was that shortly after mom's arrest. A new law office opened up in Buenos Aries. Even has the same name as my lawyer did. It's too bad they can't find him. Well at least he didn't get all of the money. Mom had half of it in her US account that was now frozen. Her new attorney is now fighting to get it released to her. She must be running up some major legal fees by now. The US attorney general has offered to release it upon her extradition back to the US. I looks like I can't touch it until then. It seems it is now need as evidence.

THE END